A Conflicted Heart
and Other Stories

❧

Charles T. Markee

A Conflicted Heart and Other Stories
by Charles T. Markee

© 2024 C. T. Markee

ISBN: 978-0-9828987-6-5

Book design by Jo-Anne Rosen

Cover art:
The Cliff House painting, completed in 1903, was an inheritance from Charles Markee's mother, Margaret Kehoe Markee. (Artist unknown)
Photo of painting by Wilson Thompson

Moonview Press
60 South 11th Street
San Jose, CA 95112

To all my grandchildren
and great-grandchildren
who will help define the future.

Contents

Introduction

The stories were inspired by my life's experiences growing up in San Francisco, experiencing the excitement working in Silicon Valley, and living in beautiful Sonoma County. Each of the stories in this book have a unique ending which I believe you will enjoy reading.

A Conflicted Heart
and Other Stories

A Conflicted Heart

Eight bells, morning, and the end of my watch. We were 22 miles east of the Farallon Islands and cruising at a steady eight knots toward the California coast. Topside, alone, and amidship, I leaned on the railing as the SS Fedora emerged from the fog bank. I stared into the water as images of Alice spun through my mind, always Alice. Would she be waiting for me?

I searched for the rational reasons I was attracted to her. Maybe it was her smile or her eyes with their translucent darkness, or maybe it was the way she flowed against me when we first danced, or possibly it was the way I knew she was there before I saw her in the room. Whatever the reason, I was overwhelmed with the stimulation and demand of my feelings. It must be love, although that single word seems inadequate.

Alice taught literature and social studies at Mission High School while I taught chemistry and technology at Sacred Heart College High, both schools in my hometown of San Francisco. Neither of us was looking for a relationship when we went to the teacher's convention in Anaheim. The hotel restaurant was packed. Rather than both waiting, I had suggested sharing a table. At first, she hesitated, but then she tilted her head as though receiving a message, smiled and agreed.

Following the waiter to our table, I experienced a surprising feeling of anticipation. Two hours later we were still talking, completely lost in finding out about each other. When I looked up, the tables were cleared and we were alone. It struck me afterwards that if I were to believe in reincarnation, I would also believe that we must have known each other before.

Both in our mid-thirties, we were an unlikely couple in appearance. Alice was black Irish, with a hint of freckles on olive skin, long dark hair she held to one side while she talked, and fine delicate features. My parents were Syrian and I had their dark complexion and prominent nose. I wasn't handsome, but I had my dad's dense stocky build and broad shoulders. I stood out in my Italian-Irish neighborhood. None of this would have predicted us as soul mates.

Alice understood me. She seemed to know what I meant without explanation. This first significant connection with a woman was exhilarating for me. I felt we were already a couple by the time we left the restaurant.

Now, she may be lost and I had done it.

A gull squawked behind me. Startled by the sound, I turned to see the wide panoramic entrance to San Francisco Bay. Two months ago I had signed on as an electronics technician and sailed out through this same Golden Gate on a cool, foggy June night. The adventure had an innocent beginning. I told my fellow teachers at a Christmas party that I was planning to spend my summer break on an oil tanker in the Pacific. It was just a casual comment, a joke really, but the story spread quickly. The farce changed from flippant remark to reality that March after the trouble began.

Alice and I had been living together for two months when we attended a friend's wedding. After the reception, Alice seemed pensive, but I thought she was just tired. That next week, we quickly submerged back into our busy schedules. Evenings were filled with paper corrections and class preparations. The following Sunday was one of those unusually clear spring days in San Francisco. Taking a break, we drove up to Twin Peaks and sat in the car for several minutes taking in the view and watching the tourists. The image of all three bridges and the East Bay hills was as crisp as an Ansel Adams photograph. Below, Market Street cut a diagonal swath, separating downtown. The view demanded our quiet, dedicated attention.

Alice pushed the car door open, got out and walked to the front of the car.

Surprised, I followed. When I moved next to her, she stiffened. I said, "What is it, honey?"

She looked straight ahead, her voice flat. "Do you believe in commitments?"

"What do you mean? Of course I do. What makes you ask?"

"Just thinking. We've known each other for a while and I wonder where it's going"

"It's going well. Aren't you happy?"

"That's not the issue, Jim. Relationships grow and develop with commitment, official commitment."

"Official?" I froze, then forced the word out. "You mean like . . . marriage?"

"Well . . . yes," she replied.

Caught off guard, I shook my head and took a step back, choosing my words carefully. "I don't think we need marriage to be committed or happy. Besides, everyone I know who gets married soon gets divorced. It's like they lose themselves as separate people and then they lose their intensity and then they lose what's special and it goes downhill from there. I don't want that to happen to us. What we have is too good."

Alice didn't respond. We stood in uncomfortable silence. I reached for her hand.

She pulled away. "Forget it. I won't bring the subject up again."

A month passed and the issue never came up. We talked and planned and made love and visited friends and went to parties, but it felt like a door had closed between us.

On the first warm spring Sunday we went for a walk in Golden Gate Park. Twists of cool air reminded me that winter had just ended. We sat on a bench overlooking Stow Lake. I put my arm around her and pulled her close. After a few minutes she said, "Jim, we need to talk."

I gave her a quizzical look. "Sure. About what?" When she didn't answer, I said, "What is it, Alice?"

"I think we should separate for a while."

"What!" I jerked my arm back. My stomach went cold. "Why?"

"We should separate . . . just to be sure."

"Be sure of what? I am sure! I love you. I want us to stay together."

"Do you?"

"Do I what?"

"Love me? Love me enough to make a commitment?"

"That again," I said, unable to control my resentment. "You said you wouldn't bring it up!"

Her eyes narrowed. "I changed my mind. It's important to me. I can't see our future if we just stay like we are." She hesitated, her mouth a thin line. "I guess it's what I've always thought about a relationship becoming . . . that is, eventually a marriage."

I was annoyed, angry and in some way I felt as though I had been tricked. Maybe she was right. Something was wrong. I felt trapped, but it wasn't Alice doing it. It was life, or was it?

The next day I spotted an ad in Sunday's Examiner for a shipboard position as an electronics technician. It was weirdly appropriate. A part of me even suspected manipulation by forces I didn't understand and a part of me remained angry. I called, interviewed and got the job. It shouldn't have been a surprise. I had done a tour in the Navy as an electronics tech and now it had secured me a summer job with Top Hat Shipping aboard the SS Fedora.

The chop—chop of helicopter blades brought me back to the present. Like a bird seeking its nest, it approached and slowed, tracking the ship's movement. The harbor pilot climbed down a rope ladder to board the ship and provide official guidance into the bay. The currents under the Golden Gate Bridge were treacherous and even a ship as large as the Fedora had to sail with caution.

On the fore deck now, I leaned on the rail and watched the Gate get closer. My time alone had been a good experience, but I was glad it was over. For two months I had buried myself in a literature potpourri: Dostoyevski, Hemingway, Chekov, Shakespeare and more, an unconscious wish to understand my own feelings about commitment and to know more about Alice, although I deliberately hadn't contacted her. Today I was leaving that hibernation. I looked down at the rolling frothy wake below and remembered how violent the sea had been during a mid-Pacific squall with 60-mile-an-hour winds, the ship pitching and the decks so slippery I feared every minute topside that I'd end up in the ocean, a severe cost for my freedom, when I could have been with Alice.

The storm already seemed like a dream from another life. It was gone now and so was my anger, the anger that I remembered as the last significant emotion between Alice and me.

I realized now that commitment was a contract for a deeper relationship. My reaction to the idea of marriage had come in large part from my brother's devastating divorce. Tom had stayed with me for a year while he struggled through it. He was left in a shambles, grieving the separation from his three children.

I hated the idea of being vulnerable and Tom's traumatic experience had had an effect on my relationship with Alice. I knew that now. Maybe I should have talked to someone about it. Instead, I had signed on for a summer at sea.

The ship was almost under the bridge. The morning sun, only slightly diminished in intensity by high clouds, rose above the Berkeley hills. The bay was already busy with morning activity, shipping to the right and a few sailboats to the left between Alcatraz and Angel Islands. I could see the traffic on the bridge. A jumbo jet climbed toward cruising altitude from the direction of San Francisco International Airport.

For the first time in two months I allowed myself to think of Alice with anticipation. I couldn't wait to see her, but I also had unrelenting surges of anxiety. I didn't know what had happened to her during these last two months. Could she have met someone else? Had her parents talked her out of considering our relationship? Was her need for separation just a way to break it off? I was awash in simultaneous conflicting emotions of fear of losing her and eagerness to see her. Had I made a mistake leaving for two months? I could hear her voice asking me, "Do you love me enough to make a commitment?"

Tourists at Fort Point watched us pass. In the hills behind the city, fog clung around the base of Sutro tower. Then a shadow from the bridge swept over the deck. I was home and I knew my answer to Alice's question.

Barefoot Cruise

Warren pulled onto Highway 17 and punched the gas in his Ford 150 pickup as he started up the winding two-lane road to the top of the mountain. Two curves later he was stuck behind one of those old VW bugs with the split back window and with 35 horsepower, and then only if the engine was tuned up.

"God damn it to hell," he swore to himself. "A fuckin' difficult 12-hour Friday and now I have to put up with this hippy joker. That's one bug I'd like to squash."

His contract as a government draftsman and site manager at Moffett Field brought in good money. But still, he resented that he had to take this day job to pay the bills. Warren was a self-starter and he liked working for himself. He just had word today from the government site manager at Fort Ord that his bid for dismantling the barracks had been accepted. He had big plans for that material and his future.

"Jesus, this guy is slow!" He flipped on his bright and tail gated the VW hoping the driver would get the hint and pull over. No such luck. "Shit!"

Twenty long grumbling minutes later, he parked under the three redwood trees in front of his house. An architect friend had created its rustic design that fit the mood of the surrounding forest. Warren was one of those rare people, a craftsman, and this house that he built himself, was a work of art.

Admiring the redwood deck, the house and the forest illuminated by the outdoor lights, he leaned on the truck, stretched his 5'10" frame and scratched his red beard. His drafting work clothes were cargo pants, a pullover shirt and running shoes.

Inside, he hung his Giant's cap on a hook by the door. "Judy? Hon? I'm home."

"I hope it's you and not some stranger walk-in' in." The sarcasm in her voice was hard to miss.

Standing in front of the range in a t-shirt and jeans with her hair in a ponytail, she didn't turn around when he came in.

"What's up, hon?" He slipped an arm around her waist.

She shook him off, "Look out. You'll get burned."

The sharp edge of her voice cut through him, "Whoa. Is this a little PMS I hear?"

She whirled around, her petite face tight and crimson. "Don't get funny with me, Warren. You ever hear of telephones? Where the hell were you that you couldn't call me. It's almost ten o'clock. I've been waiting dinner for four hours."

He glared back at her, "What's the matter with you? You know how it is with these deadlines. I had to finish today. Gimme a break!"

She ignored him and dropped two small steaks in a skillet as Warren grabbed a Heineken from the fridge and popped it open. "Stick those two potatoes in the microwave, Warren." And she banged the spatula on the iron skillet to emphasize her command.

He clamped his mouth shut to keep from saying anything, stabbed some vicious holes in the potatoes with a fork, set them on a plate and put them in the microwave for three minutes. Leaning against the wall and watching Judy cook, he knew he was in the wrong, but he didn't want to back down. With her jaw set tight, he knew she wouldn't back down either. It was going to be an ugly dinner unless he did something and the ball was in his court. Finally he said, "You're right, hon. I shoulda called you."

She leaned on the range and looked him in the eye, "Is that an apology?"

"Yeah," he said. "It's an apology. I'm sorry I didn't call."

Her shoulders relaxed and the tightness slipped out of her face, "Okay, let's eat."

The table in the kitchen gave them a view of the trees through screened windows open to let in the late evening spring breeze. With dinner plates pushed aside, Judy swirled her remaining half glass of red wine and Warren nursed his second Heineken.

Judy said, "Today, I ..."

At the same time, Warren said, "This week ..."

They both stopped and laughed. Warren said, "Go ahead."

She said, "No, you started. You go ahead."

"Okay. I won the government bid. It's the break I've been waiting for. With the material from those buildings, I can build the home we've been talking about on the view lot above us. When it's done, we can sell this house, pay off the construction loan and own the new house free and clear." He reached across and took her hand, "With no mortgage, you can quit your job. It's our dream come true."

She pulled her hand away, "I don't want to quit my job, Warren. Database management is challenging and I'm good at it. Besides, we need to set aside some money for retirement."

"Yeah. Okay. You're right again, hon, but the pressure will be off."

She gave him a sidelong glance. "When does this project at RT start?"

"That's the sweet thing about this. My contract is up on May 30, and I have to start demolition on June 1st. It's perfect timing. I already called Danny, Jim and Sam. They're ready to go on June 1st. I took a break at work in order to arrange all this, and that's why I had to work late. I was so stoked that I worked overtime and finished drafting my heat pipe design. I just didn't think to phone you."

Warren leaned back in his chair with a smile like the Cheshire cat in Alice in Wonderland. Judy studied him, her face impassive. Why wasn't she responding to all this good news? His smile drooped, then disappeared. He leaned forward, "What's the matter, hon?"

"June 1st."

"Yes," he said. "That's when we start. What about it?"

"You don't remember?"

"Remember what?" he asked.

She shook her head and looked at her glass of wine. He waited, curious and confused. She slowly raised her head and said, "Our romantic cruise, Warren. The cruise we booked six months ago. The good deal we got, a two for one price for booking early."

"Oh." He said.

"That's all you have to say, is oh?"

"I remember," he said, brightening. "It was called Windjammer."

"Yes, Windjammer Barefoot Cruises. They have four sailing ships and we chose the Yankee Clipper. We board at Grand Bahama Island on June 1st."

"Un, oh," he said. "I can't do June 1st. We'll have to reschedule."

"No, Warren. You'll have to reschedule."

"It was a government bid. I can't reschedule or I'll default and lose the contract."

She shrugged. Her eyebrows rose, as if to say, this is a no brainer. Anyone with an ounce of sense would go on the cruise. He frowned, dilemma shaping his countenance. She could almost see the gears inside his head turning. Finally, he said, "You'll have to go alone."

She crunched up her face, incredulous, "You're kidding."

"No. It's okay," he said. "You can go. I have to stay here to start the contract. The guys are depending on me. It'll be alright. You can tell me about it when you get back."

She stared at him, "You're sure?"

"No problem."

She stood up. "You're absolutely sure?"

He nodded, "Yup."

June 1st rolled around, Judy flew to the Caribbean and Warren started his contract at Fort Ord. To save time, he rented a room for a week in Monterey with Sam. There was no sense commuting an hour and fifteen minutes each way and he hated coming home to an empty house. Judy would pop into his mind now and then and he wondered about the cruise, but he shoved the thoughts away and concentrated on his new self-employed career and the house he was going to build. He missed her, but it was no big deal.

At the end of the week on the drive home from the Monterey Peninsula, his iPhone sounded a ringtone for an incoming call. It was Judy calling.

Her voice bubbled with enthusiasm. "The cruise was terrific. I had a wonderful time. I'm just calling to tell you my plane will be in San Jose about 1:30 pm tomorrow and Warren ..."

He waited and when she didn't say anything he said, "What, Judy?"

"Things have changed."

"Just a minute." He negotiated the exchange from Hwy 156 onto Hwy 101, north bound.

"I'm back," he said. "What do you mean, things have changed. What's changed?"

After another long pause, she said, "I'm moving out."

"What?" He wasn't sure he heard correctly. "What did you say?"

"I'm moving out, Warren. Stan and I have to catch our planes now. Bye."

The line went dead.

Billy Ray

B illy Ray Sanders hated Clarence Harris. There was
no two ways about it. And it wasn't one of those
passing dislikes or flash furies that hit you and then
you went on about your business. This hate wound
all through Billy Ray's body, existed in every part of
him, from his skin all the way through to his guts. It
was always churning in there rising like bile in his
throat whenever Clarence drove into his gas station.

This was a slow day, like most all the days in
Littleville, Texas and Billy Ray sat in his station with
his feet up on the Titan electric heater working on a cup
of grungy coffee. He had a brake job up on the rack,
but it could wait for him to smoke his Camel while he
thought about how much he hated Clarence. He even
hated thinking about how much he hated Clarence.

Strange to recall now, but he and Clarence had
been best friends at Littleville High; played together
on the basketball and football teams and both ran
track. When they graduated, Billy Ray stayed in
Littleville working at this dad's gas station, while
Clarence went off to college in Southern California.
Billy Ray and Sue became a thing while he was gone.
Most everyone in town figured they'd be gettin' married and as far as Billy Ray was concerned, it was a
done deal. She was his. Then Clarence came back.

Billy Ray didn't realize anything at first. Why should he? Clarence was busy getting a loan and starting up his pizza business across the street. There were a lot of changes going on in that building across the street where there used to be an ice cream shop. Now there were new booths, tables, counters and ovens. He saw Sue talking with Clarence, but it wasn't unusual. Everyone was stopping by the place to see what he was doing. And she'd always come back across the street to his station to talk to him afterwards.

Then suddenly, Clarence was open for business. Billy Ray could smell the pizza cooking all the way across the street. He was surprised at how fast people took to it. The pizza shop became the town hang out and he noticed Sue going in there more and more, so he talked to her about it.

"Sue, I don't like you hanging around that pizza place so much."

"Clarence wants me to help him in there."

"What do ya mean help him?"

"You know, like a waitress. It's gotten so busy; he can't do it all himself."

"You don't need a job, Sue."

"I want to do it, Billy. It's the most exciting thing in town and Clarence needs the help."

Billy Ray looked at her. She had a new flush of determination he hadn't seen before and he didn't like it, "I don't want you workin' in there, Sue."

She put both hands on her hips and looked him in the eye, "You don't rule me, Billy Ray. I suppose you expect me to stay over here with you in this smelly old grease pit. You got another thing comin' if you think that."

She turned, walked out and across the street and straight into the pizza shop. Billy Ray fumed, kicked the wastebasket out the front door and paced around for an hour before he could get calm enough to do any work.

That was just the beginning. Billy Ray's life went from bad to terrible in a hurry. The next time he called Sue, she put him off. Then he heard from his hunting buddies, Slim and Nicky Boy that she had been seen with Clarence driving out of town one evening. That weekend, Sue called him and broke it off.

"Billy Ray, honey, it jus' ain't workin' out."

"You're seeing that God damn Clarence, right?"

"That's my business, Billy Ray."

"BANG!" He slammed the phone down so hard it almost broke the plastic cradle. He grabbed the office chair and threw it into the shop, then stormed around kicking anything loose, "son-of-bitch, son-of-bitch, son-of-bitch, son-of-a-fuckin'-bitch!"

It wasn't too long before Sue and Clarence got married. It was then that Billy Ray got sour and stayed sour. If his gas station weren't the only gas in town, people would've stopped going there, because he always looked like he was about to chew on the gas cap.

The pizza shop stayed the busiest shop in town, right across the street from Billy Ray, where he had to look at it every day and he had to look at Sue going in there every day. And it seemed like Clarence could do no wrong. He added Gelato, and that was a hit. He became more active in the community and was voted on the town council. Billy Ray stopped going; nobody listened to him anyhow. Everybody loved Clarence and Billy Ray hated him all the more.

One June day, he didn't see Sue going into the pizza shop. That evening Nicky Boy wandered by, "Hey, Billy. You gotta smoke on you?"

Billy snarled, "You ever buy your own?"

"Not if I can help it. You look in a pissy mood."

Billy Ray snatched his pack of cigs off the counter. "What's up with Sue Harris?"

"What do you mean?"

"She's not workin'. She sick?'

"Nope. Pregnant."

A frown pressed Billy Ray's forehead like a dark cloud. "Fuck!"

"What you care for?"

"Shut the fuck up, Nicky!"

The baby boy was big news. He was John Clarence Harris, named for his grandfather and his dad and he became the town favorite. Clarence and now his boy seemed to fall into roses every time they turned around.

In contrast, like the Portrait of Dorian Gray, Billy Ray began to look as evil as he felt inside. His hands were permanently greasy, he rarely shaved, and he cut his own hair in the mirror. The wrinkles of a plastered frown pressed his eyes into a mean squint.

John grew up, and like his dad, seemed to excel with little effort. He was accepted at UC Berkeley and went off to college in California as a business major. The whole town followed his progress. Clarence kept his picture in the shop window with a running record of his grade point average posted for all to see. Billy Ray watched through his binoculars from across the street.

John came home during spring break of his senior year. It was that visit that pushed Billy Ray over the edge. He, Slim and Nicky Boy were sitting on milk crates behind the station drinking beer and smoking. A case of Coors sat on the ground between them.

Slim popped his third can; pulled out a smoke, turned to Billy Ray and said, "Light me up."

"Light your fuckin' self."

"Whoa! What's eatin' you Billy?"

"Didn't you see it?"

"What?"

"You blind! That there flashing red neon sign."

Slim looked at him, "What sign?"

Nicky Boy turned to Slim." The one flashing 'Pizza.' Bone head."

Billy Ray pulled another beer from the case, popped it open, "We gotta do something about it."

Nicky Boy looked at Slim, then turned to Billy Ray, "What we gonna do?"

Billy's voice growled low, "Burn 'em!"

"Burn em?" they said in shocked unison.

"Yeah," Billy continued, "Burn 'em out and it's gotta be an accident."

No one seemed to know how the fire started that night. By the time anyone noticed, the pizza shop glowed like a giant ember where yellow flames had burned it to the ground. The volunteers were able to save the buildings on either side, but the pizza shop was totaled.

The next day, Billy Ray was hanging around the station with Nicky Boy and Slim when he spotted Clarence driving slowly down the street toward him. He chuckled to himself, a rare thing. "Here comes the poor shit, now," he said as he greeted Clarence with a smirk.

Clarence pulled his new Mercedes SUV in next to a pump. Thumbs tucked in his belt, Billy Ray strode up to the driver side window. "Having a good day? Heh, heh, heh."

Clarence leaned out his window and said, "Came to get gas and say goodbye, Billy Ray."

"Goodbye?" Billy Ray's face dropped.

Clarence got outa the car, started pumping gas, "Yep. It's our dream come true. A million five in fire insurance on that place sets us up for life. John and his wife have enough money to stay here and rebuild the Pizza shop. We were already tired of the place, and wanted to retire to New Mexico, but couldn't see a way to do it. Now it's a dream come true. We're on our way today."

Billy Ray saw Sue wave from the passenger side, but he didn't move.

Clarence put the hose away, put the gas cap back on and walked back to the driver's door. He pulled out a twenty, "Here Billy, keep it. Forget the past." Then he got in and drove away.

Billy Ray gaped as the twenty-dollar bill left his hand and floated to the ground.

Blackberry Pie

Herman Weinkauf liked routine, familiar locations and things in their proper place. He didn't know when it started, this penchant for orderliness, but it was so much a part of his life now, that he took it for granted. So, the man sitting at the corner table that was usually vacant, bothered him.

The Oakville Grocery and gourmet snack shop in Healdsburg was part of Herman's routine. He would leave his small accounting business office that was right off the town square promptly at 11:30 am, walk one block, cross the street to Oakville on the corner and order his usual tomato bisque soup with a half tuna salad sandwich on a French roll. He loved this store with its wonderful gourmet deli that used all fresh ingredients. The bisque had a slight tang and was so sumptuous that it always gave Herman a little shiver of pleasure as the first spoonful touched his tongue.

There was also a wine and coffee bar in the grocery and part of his daily lunch routine included a glass of Lambert Bridge sauvignon blanc. It didn't exactly go with the bisque, but it complemented the tuna perfectly. To adjust for that, he set the wine aside while he slowly and luxuriously spooned the soup into his mouth. Then he cleared his pallet with a drink of water and ate the sandwich and drank the wine together.

Yesterday when he first noticed the man, Herman had carried his soup, sandwich, and wine to the outdoor seating, which looked out on the intersection of Matheson and Center Streets. He liked one table in particular that was under an umbrella and gave him a nice view of the intersection with its crosswalks. The people and cars were constant entertainment and he enjoyed watching the pedestrians, some in couples, some alone and some with dogs. It was, he thought, just like sitting at a street café in Paris.

He had finished his soup and set the bowl aside, when he became aware again of the man sitting in the corner next to the outdoor fireplace. There was an empty plate and fork in front of him and the man's chair was pushed back, so he was almost invisible under the shade of the umbrella that conveniently shaded his iPad. A puff of the chilly October breeze flapped the umbrella, but he didn't put it down. He probably wasn't hiding there, but it seemed like it, because Herman had the eerie feeling he was being watched.

As Herman ate his sandwich, he took occasional sips of wine and every time he did, he'd glance over to see if the man was still reading his iPad. As he took the last bite of his sandwich, he reminded himself that it was completely inconsequential who the man was or what he was doing there. He was a total stranger sitting nowhere near Herman. There was no justification for any suspicions about the man. After all, he hadn't made a move during the half hour that Herman was there, and he couldn't even tell what the man looked like. Nevertheless, Herman couldn't stop thinking about him. And, in fact, he did wonder what he looked like.

The seats were filling up now that it was the noon hour and the experience of solitude was rapidly vanishing, so Herman stood up and prepared to leave. He bussed his plate and glass to the outdoor counter set up for that purpose and he deliberately took a path through the tables so he could see the man. But just as he was about to get a glimpse under the edge of the umbrella, the man decided to reach up and adjust the umbrella. This lowered the edge of the umbrella, further hiding him, and Herman would have had to stand there waiting and staring to see him. Of course, he couldn't do that. He muttered a "damn!" to himself and left in a huff.

The next morning's work was dreadful. It seemed that all the most irascible clients converged on him during that one morning. Every exchange had been fraught with tension and Herman was so rattled by the morning's office experiences that he left for his Oakville lunch five minutes earlier than usual, a welcome escape. When he reached the street intersection, he noticed again that the city had replaced the orderly control of traffic lights with arterial stop signs. He grumbled to himself about stupid community decisions and started across the street after he was sure that all the cars had stopped and had seen him. Halfway across the street he spotted the man sitting at the corner table and stopped dead. In the turmoil of the morning, he had forgotten about the man and now it all rushed back into his consciousness.

The man was there with his iPad again and sitting in the same corner.

A car horn beeped, and Herman jumped. He was standing in the middle of the street blocking the intersection. He could see the driver behind the wheel waving a fist at him, so he hurried across the street and didn't look back for fear the angry driver might get out of the car and make his morning even worse than it already was.

Herman went through his routine food and wine purchase automatically. What was this man doing there behind the umbrella? He chastised himself for becoming so obsessed, but he couldn't stop himself.

As he walked to an alternate table, he noticed something different. The man had a piece of blackberry pie on a plate in front of him, however he was still reading his iPad in the shade and Herman still couldn't see him. As he sat down, he remembered his childhood and his love for blackberry pie. He and his grandmother had picked blackberries together by the creek that ran behind her house. Then she had made a blackberry pie for him, and it had become his favorite dessert as a child. He hadn't tasted blackberry pie for years and the thought of it made his mouth water.

He sat down and took a quick drink of his wine, forgetting his routine. He had the bisque and ate the sandwich, furtively glancing at the corner hoping the man would tip his umbrella, but he never did. As Herman left Oakville, he realized that he had spent all his time trying to see the man behind the umbrella and never watching the people crossing the intersection like he normally did. He couldn't even remember finishing his lunch. His carefree Oakville visit had fallen victim to his obsession about the mysterious man behind the umbrella. This was all very unsettling and not at all orderly.

That evening, Herman decided he needed a drink, an alcoholic drink. He rummaged around in the basement looking for the liqueur that he remembered his grandmother stored there. Finally, he found it, an old, very dusty, unopened bottle of Bailey's Irish Cream. In his kitchen, he broke the seal and removed the cork top with a pop. A quick rush of smoky vapor escaped that smelled a little like star jasmine. Weird, he thought, but he was in no mood for analysis. He didn't have any liqueur glasses, so he poured about three fingers of the creamy liquid into a small water glass and took it off to his bedroom where he read himself to sleep.

He knew this was a dream because he felt a complete freedom from his routine. Time for change. He looked at his watch and it was early, barely 10 am. Good, he thought, I'll get there before he does. Herman stood up from his desk and floated through the wall of his office. Outside, he took long loping dream steps toward Oakville, passing people on the sidewalk with no faces. He moved like the astronauts on the moon. There were no cars in the intersection as he crossed it in two floating steps, went quickly into the Oakville grocery and approached the deli counter. He spotted the blackberry pie in a display case and imagined the berry juice in his mouth. He bought a piece. Outside he found the other man's chair at the corner table, pushed it back against the wall, adjusted the umbrella and sat down. Now, he thought, he can't avoid me, and I'll finally get to see what he looks like. He quickly ate the blackberry pie, savoring each bite, and pushed the plate away. He opened his iPad, started to read and waited.

The Oakville store door swung open, and he watched himself walk to his favorite table with a tray loaded with tomato bisque, a tuna salad sandwich, a glass of Lambert Bridge sauvignon blanc and a slice of blackberry pie.

Change

Christmas Eve shoppers hurried past Harry Stafford, who sat slumped on a bench in the shopping mall. He clutched a paper cup of coffee he had purchased at the kiosk and stared at the ground under his feet. He ignored the tinsel, the lights, the garland—and the music from overhead speakers, as the vocalist began singing, "Chestnuts roasting in an open fire…" He set the coffee cup down on the bench, ran his fingers through his white hair, took off his glasses and rubbed his eyes. With his glasses on, he could see the wrinkles and liver spots on the back of his hands.

Harry felt foolish losing the money he had just drawn from his account. His daughter had dropped him at the bank so he could deposit his Social Security check. When he had his own business, before he retired, he was proud of his memory, his accuracy and his ability to keep track of details. Now details slipped away, and sometimes, he even forgot what he was doing. Worst of all, he lost things. This was Christmas Eve, the wrong time to lose a gift for his granddaughter. He frowned with the pain of it.

His daughter had driven him to the shopping mall near his independent living apartment so he could go to the bank while she shopped. He had walked with purpose using his cane and enjoyed all the happy people intent on their shopping—children were hardly able to contain themselves and teens chatted on their cell phones. That seemed strange to Harry, like they were talking to themselves.

At the bank, when it was his turn at the counter, he leaned toward the clerk, handed him a withdrawal slip and whispered, "I'd like to have a hundred dollar bill, please. It's a gift for my granddaughter. She's a high school senior and she's saving for college."

The clerk looked down at the slip and typed in the account number. He looked up with a smile and said, "That will be no problem, Mr. Stafford."

Harry said, "Can you make it a crisp bill?" He took the brand new currency, folded it neatly in half and put it in his pocket. It always felt a little more like Christmas when he knew he had a gift to give someone, and his granddaughter, Sarah, was his favorite.

Harry had then walked back to the bench where he had planned to meet his daughter. He sat, put his coffee aside and reached in his pocket for the $100 dollar bill…but it was gone. He blurted, "Oh my God! I must have dropped it. If somebody sees it they'll just take it." But when he retraced his steps, there was no bill.

Harry could not afford another $100. He felt Christmas had been destroyed and he could do nothing but wait on the bench, heart sick, until his daughter returned.

Twenty minutes later, she walked up. "Dad! What's the matter?"

"I lost the gift," he said. His eyes started to water although he fought it.

Just then, someone tapped on his back.

"Excuse me, sir." Harry looked up at a young man who had appeared out of the crowd. "I'm glad I found you. You forgot your change."

"Change?" Harry seemed puzzled.

"Yes. Change for the $100 dollar bill you used to pay for your coffee." "Merry Christmas," he said, as he handed Harry the money.

Cliff House

The seven o'clock mass had concluded at Our Lady of Lourdes Church in San Francisco and Charles Kehoe was beginning his usual walk home, when he decided to visit the new Cliff House. The idea simply popped into his head, a very unlikely thought for him to have, being a regular fellow and not normally given to such merry thoughts. However, the weather was particularly appealing this September Sunday with crisp cool air and bright sun shining through infrequent puffs of cloud.

Following mass, his Sundays were usually spent in the garden, caring for his roses, and tending to the vegetables he had planted in the spring: tomatoes, string beans, squash, onions, and potatoes. Afternoon was a time for reading history books borrowed from the local free library and read assiduously from cover to cover. Thus employed, he never considered himself lonely.

Already wearing his bowler hat, long coat, and boots, he retrieved his walking stick from his home and strode toward Market Street and the Ferry Building to catch the Sutor Railroad trolley to the beach. This was quite an adventure for him. Not the walk of course, for he was an intrepid walker, but the day trip across town.

As he walked along the city streets, he nodded to the gentlemen, tipped his hat to unescorted women, and looked past couples so as not to intrude. He mused over who these people were, what they were doing and where they were going. It was a mental game he played in lieu of actually meeting them. It didn't bother him that he had no close friends, men, or women. His routine was all the engagement he needed, and he fully expected that when he reached a marriageable age, a female friendship would develop. Irishmen in his family typically married in their 30s or 40s.

He was tall, nearly six feet, with sloped shoulders and complexion ruddy from his work outdoors as a postman. At 27 years of age, he already had salt and pepper hair and heavy eyebrows that ran together. With his long legs and habitual rapid walk, he quickly reached Market Street.

The nickel railroad fare was an extravagance on his salary. But he reconciled himself to the cost, remembering that the expenditure was for the round trip. He had been reading about the newest Cliff House ever since its reconstruction by the wealthy ex-San Francisco mayor, Adolph Sutor, known locally as the King of the Comstock. The Cliff House had quickly become a celebrated tourist destination. Many neighbors along his mail route had already visited this Cliff House and highly praised the experience. Without realizing it, his anticipation had grown with each telling, so it was no wonder that the idea had popped into his head on this lovely Sunday.

Elated by his ride on the electric trolley, Charles memorized every vision: glimpses of the bay, sailing ships at the entrance to the bay and the surprising number of new homes. The smell of salty ocean air foretold the end of the line before the conductor announced it.

He hurried out of the Sutro Depot building and stopped mid-stride, stunned by the site of the Sutro Bath and Museum. The complex looked like a gigantic greenhouse, Victorian in style and constructed with 100,000 panes of sparkling crystal glass. When it had opened eight years ago, in 1896, the local Examiner newspaper claimed that its salt-water pools could accommodate 1,600 bathers.

Charles was curious, but also frugal. It cost 25 cents to swim and 10 cents to observe, neither of which he was willing to pay even if they did provide bathing costumes and towels. Besides, he was eager to see the new Cliff House.

As Charles stood to one side, savoring the scene, several excited young women left the depot and started toward the Baths followed by their circumspect gentlemen friends. Half a dozen grade schoolboys had dismounted at the same time and with the enthusiasm of their age, rapidly passed the adults while pushing and shoving each other. A separate larger group including men, women, and a few couples, exited the depot and turned toward the Cliff House, which was further down the hill on a gravel roadway and visible across from a cliff that rose a hundred feet straight up to the Sutro Mansion.

Sutro's new Cliff House was astounding, a veritable fairyland palace painted white with round towers at each corner, several gables looking out from the pink roof and a central tower rising at least four stories above the ground. Its perch on the rocky ledge over a steep drop-off to the Pacific Ocean added to the impression of it being a fantasy castle.

As Charles stepped off from the depot, a strong breeze off the ocean whipped his coat around his legs and forced him to hold onto his hat brim for fear it would take leave of his head. A woman walking alone in front of him reached up to grasp her wide-brimmed hat, which was flapping in the gust, but she was too late. She uttered a distressed, "Oh, dear!" as it took flight directly toward Charles and bounced in front of him. He reached down and grabbed for it but holding his own hat with one hand and his walking stick with the other, he missed, and it rolled on its brim like a child's hoop up the hill toward the depot. Charles, being quite nimble, had no trouble jogging up the hill and retrieving the hat, which he returned, only a little out of breath.

As he handed her the hat, he looked down into her pretty blue eyes and a round face that held a delightful smile. She said, "Oh, thank you, sir. It's my favorite." She sparkled with an enthusiasm that colored her cheeks and he blushed in response. Seemingly unaware of his discomfort, she continued in a self-deprecating tone, "I should have tied its ribbon. I must be more careful next time, don't you think?" When he didn't reply, she started back down the hill toward the Cliff House, a slight bounce in her step.

Charles stood entranced, watching her, and remembering the lyrical sound of her voice. He wondered why she was alone and how old she was. He started down the hill, but in his mind's eye, he kept seeing her smile, her blue dress with the lace collar and her auburn hair in curls. Why hadn't he said anything to her? He felt a distinct regret, dismayed at having missed an opportunity. He replayed the event in his thoughts contributing wit to his imaginary conversation. But, no! He was being too frivolous. Unused to such fantasizing, he shook his head to clear his thoughts. After all, saving her hat was just a friendly gesture, nothing more. Naturally she'd been grateful. It was, after all, her favorite hat.

Resuming his trek, he recalled reading that an earlier expanded version of the first building, referred to as the second Cliff House, had been partially demolished by the explosion of 42 tons of black powder carried aboard the good ship *Parallel*, which had foundered on the rocks below. Later, the building had burned to the ground because of a chimney fire. Sutro had completed this third building in the style of an opulent French chalet in the same year his Baths were opened.

On the path in front, Charles slowed his walk to study the architecture of the building. People were visible at several of the windows, but he became more curious about the ocean side from which he could already hear waves crashing on the rocks below intermingled with the raucous barking of sea lions. The seaside balconies would be accessed through the lobby. He paused, somewhat intimidated by the grandeur, but his curiosity prevailed, and he pushed open the large double doors into a foyer where each footstep sank into the deep rich maroon carpeting. Every surface shined and the room smelled like pipe smoke and new furniture. He glanced around nervously.

Well-dressed couples with suitcases were checking in at a long-polished wood reception counter on his left. In the expansive lobby, gentlemen sat in leather chairs, smoking and reading the morning paper. Ladies sipped tea and chatted.

A young man in a blue bellhop uniform approached him, "May I help you, sir?"

Charles stood tall and pulled his shoulders back hoping that he appeared more elegant than he felt. He thought about his well-worn shirt and trousers and was relieved that his relatively new long coat covered them. "Yes," he said. "I'd like to see the ocean view from your balcony."

"Right this way." The bellhop wheeled around, motioned toward the rear of the room and set off at a quick pace, the shiny stripe down his pant leg flashing with each step. Charles followed through double doors, each inset with a stained-glass image of an ocean sunset. They tread silently down the plush carpet of the long hallway. Framed photographs of sailing ships decorating the walls on either side. At the end of the hall, a heavy wooden door, inset with a modest porthole opened onto the balcony. Charles reached in his pocket and dropped a penny into the Bellhop's outstretched hand pretending that he didn't see his frown.

Charles removed his hat and stepped toward the banister where the sight took his breath away. Three stories below, waves crashed against rugged rocks and thrust up out of the water like miniature mountains. Beyond, the vast Pacific Ocean disappeared into the horizon. With the ocean breeze in his face and the wind whipping through his hair, he imagined for a moment that he was the captain of an ocean liner.

He had never been on such a ship, but he thought it must be thrilling. In fact, simply standing there was thrilling.

Testing the banister first, he peered over the edge and toyed with the idea of his imaginary ship sinking or the balcony giving way and falling to the rocks below ... then he canceled those thoughts and glanced to the right and left. Couples on either side of him stood close to each other enjoying the same view and embracing in an intimate way. The word honeymoon flashed through his mind.

Movement on the closest of two small islands of rock caught his eye as a sea lion slid into the water. Another, disturbed by the splash, barked and was answered by others on both rocks. The antics of the seal lions and the rolling waves capping and beating against the island rocks hypnotized Charles. He inhaled the salt air and thought about the contrast between this small adventure and the routine of his life. His job as a postman brought him outdoors Monday through Saturday, providing him with rigorous exercise climbing the San Francisco hills as well as the society of the good people on his route. He recalled the day that President McKinley was shot. Many on his route waited for him so they could discuss the medical reports as the president lingered on and then died. That had been the most exceptional day on his route. He compared that day to the exciting and impulsive experience today. That day on his route had been engaging, but today stimulated his sense of adventure.

"Why, hello again."

He recognized the musical voice before he saw her

and snapped out of his reverie. "Hello," he croaked, with a strangled voice.

She rested one gloved hand on the banister next to him and cocked her head, "It's delightful, isn't it? I love this view and what a lovely day."

"Yes." His mind churned. He wanted to say more, something to keep her here, but his brain scrambled, and he felt the heat of a blush on his cheeks.

She frowned, "Are you all right?"

"Yes, yes," he stuttered. "Just surprised." Again, he couldn't think of anything intelligent to say. The silence hung between them like an unanswered question. Why couldn't he think? He chatted every day with people on his route. This shouldn't be so hard. He knew how to make conversation.

"I know," she said with a sly grin. "You're concerned because we haven't been introduced. Well, we're two adults in this modern age. We can introduce ourselves. I'll be first." She offered her right kid-gloved hand and automatically, he took it. The shock of it hit him, her eyes, the touch of her hand. He couldn't move. Slowly she smiled and with feigned formality, said, "My name is Irene Curran and I'm glad to make your acquaintance."

She was Irish! The recognition struck him as soon as he heard her last name. The pug nose, the pleasant happy-go-lucky countenance, the sprinkle of freckles below her eyes and her auburn hair. It all gave him an instant sense of connection.

"Well," she said, retrieving her hand and placing both hands on her hips. "It's your turn to be introducing yourself, it is."

He smiled at her Irish phrasing. "Ahhh, yes." He

coughed, gathering his fractured thoughts. "I'm sorry. My name is Charles Kehoe, Charles Edward Kehoe. I live in the Bayview District and I'm … I'm a postman."

"That's nice," she said. "I think being a postman is nice."

Another painful pause. He knew it was his turn to talk, to share in the responsibility of the conversation. What to say? He asked, "Do you live in San Francisco, Miss Curran?"

"I do and please call me Irene."

"Oh, yes, of course, Irene." Uttering her name gave him an unexpected jolt of pleasure.

"And may I call you, Charles?"

"Oh. Yes, yes, please do."

"Good," she said. "How long have you lived here?"

"All my life. I was born here," he answered, "although my father was born in Ireland."

She brightened, "Mine, too."

More comfortable now, he said, "Have you been here before? To the Baths or to the Cliff House?"

She shook her head, "Never. The idea of visiting the Cliff House just popped into my head after church this morning. My mother didn't want me to come without a chaperone, but I argued until she had to let me or listen to my complaining. Can you imagine? Twenty-six years old and she still thinks I need a chaperone. Why would anyone bother an old maid like me?" Charles could think of no appropriate comment, so he didn't say anything. She continued, "This was also my first-time riding on Mr. Sutro's trolley. I thought it was noisy and a little fast, a very rough ride. It was terrible the way we were jostled and thrown into each other. Don't you agree?"

"Well, I'm sure the Wright brothers went faster in their flying machine."

He instantly regretted the remark, her blank look worse than a condemnation. She certainly doesn't care one nit about flying machines. Recovering, he said, "Never mind. I don't think that flying idea will ever amount to much."

She laughed, "You're right about that, Charles. It's altogether a silly idea."

He glanced around and noticed that the other couples had left. He tensed. How strange. Other couples. He had automatically thought of Irene and himself as a couple. Couple to him denoted marriage. The shock of the idea overwhelmed him, as though he had touched a door that had always been locked. What did it mean? Of course, he had assumed that he might meet a woman someday, but that would be in the future.

Lost in thought, watching the ocean, he didn't notice that she was staring at him. When he did, he shifted uncomfortably, knowing that she expected him to do something, but he had not the faintest idea what.

She drew out the sound of his name, "Charles."

"Yes."

"Soon, I must take the trolley home. I'd like to visit the beach."

"You would?"

She waited.

He waited, confused. Why didn't she say more? She wanted something. The moment stretched as a buoyant thought slowly rose to the surface of his consciousness. "Ahhhh," he said. "Miss Curran, would you accompany me for a short walk on the beach?"

"I would be delighted, Mr. Kehoe."

As he turned back toward the double doors into the lobby, he offered his arm and she moved next to him and slid her arm into his.

The path down to the beach was steep and she held his arm the whole way. He was nonplussed, yet strangely ebullient and incredibly proud to have her on his arm. As they moved down onto the sandy beach, she removed her shoes, then turned to him, "It's a bit risqué to remove one's shoes, but they simply fill with sand anyway."

He smiled, "No one will notice, and I won't tell a soul, I promise." They had only walked a short distance when Charles raised his walking stick and pointed it out to sea. "Look there. A sloop is traveling upwind and tacking toward the beach."

"How does a postman know about sailing?" She asked.

"I know only a little really, but I've always been fascinated by sailing ships. I read Richard Henry Dana's *Two Years before the Mast* twice, from cover to cover." They strolled silently along the beach. At one point, he glanced back toward the pathway and noticed a man under the hood behind a tripod and camera. "Oh! We've just been photographed. I wonder if a copy might be available?"

Trudging through the sand, they reached the photographer as he slipped out from under his hood. Charles inquired, "By chance, sir, did you catch us in a previous picture?"

He answered, "I believe, I did. Were you pointing your walking stick?"

"Indeed, I was. Can I obtain a copy from you?"

"I use photographs to create paintings for sale."

Irene exclaimed, "Oh, Charles, a painting would be lovely!"

The photographer added, "My paintings are on mahogany tree sections. The price is 10 cents, but they will last forever."

It was more than Charles would otherwise spend, but he felt a strange new exuberance about the day, the painting, and Irene.

~

Two years later, he and Irene Curran were married in Our Lady of Lourdes Church. That painting, possibly my grandfather and grandmother standing on the beach below the Cliff House in 1904, hangs on the wall of my library.

Conan

I'm caged up for three weeks, my reward for being a hero. And, just my luck, it's also a busy vacation week, so the kennel is jam-packed. The only space left for me, an extra-large German shepherd, was a small cage where I could barely turn around. However, thanks to their kennel policy, I got to run in an outdoor area twice a day.

They call me Conan. My partner, Jimmy, named me after the comedian Conan O'Brien, but I think of myself as "Conan the Irish mythological hero." Jimmy and I work as a team and he thought it would be clever to have a partner with a name that went with his name, Jimmy O'Brien. It was also conveniently the name of an Irish Superhero. I suppose it's better than some other possible names.

Jimmy's first thought had been Captain America, which I would have hated. I was sure glad when he decided against the name of a movie hero. Then, he really liked Cyrano, but he wasn't so sure that the people we worked with would even know who Cyrano de Bergerac was. Of course, it might fit because Cyrano was famous for his nose.

Since Conan O'Brien was his father's favorite comedian, that cinched it. We were paired. I'm not sure I like the name, but I'm sure you know how things work. Once a name gets started, it's impossible to change.

Jimmy and I do interdiction work, primarily narcotics. We detect an assortment of schedule 1 and 2 drugs including heroin, marijuana, opium, methamphetamine, cocaine and crack cocaine. Occasionally we get called for firearms, munitions or explosives detection, but those jobs are rare, and they can be more dangerous.

We got our start together in New York, working for an organization that contracted with schools and businesses that wanted to insure they had drug free environments. It was a good experience, but we wanted to come to California and we also wanted to be independent. So, with four years of experience, a strong reputation and good connections established, we made the leap.

California has been great. I hated trudging through snow in New York, so the weather in California was a big plus for me. From the start, we got more work than we expected. Our connections from the east coast led us to companies and schools, but we also got work in airports. It was in an airport that I did the most important interdiction of my life and it's also why I'm stuck in this noisy kennel for the next three weeks. Some reward!

Jimmy is my "alpha" person, so I'm not going to knock him or his work, but this kennel is not my idea of a good time. After all, I'm a Hornbeck graduate with special training in eleven explosive odors, even though our interdiction specialty so far in California has only been narcotics.

On the day that everything happened, there was a suspected narcotics runner arriving at one of the larger California airports. I won't reveal its name in order to maintain some security about our operations. Our contract with the airport security management people provides call-in service for suspected narcotic smuggling whenever they get a notice from the NEA, Narcotic Enforcement Association. For this job, we met the plane and checked out the suspect and his carry-on, then went to the baggage area where we met the local airport security people. I carefully sniffed out his stored luggage. I've got one of the best noses in the business and this guy was clean, so we were finished for the day.

It was a quick contract job, so Jim dropped off an invoice at the business office and we started for our car. The management offices were on the third floor so we had to go down one floor and through the arrival and departure areas to reach the bridge over to the parking garage. The place was huge, and it was crowded. You have to be a dog to understand odor overload, but this was it; multi-ethnic, multi-cuisine, and packages of everything. There were babies in diapers (yuk!), unwashed homeless guys and some of the most offensive colognes and perfumes you could imagine. It was one of those days when I longed for a nice telephone pole. Humans think that dogs have a special attraction to fire hydrants, but that's just a myth propagated by the guys who like to paint fire hydrants.

We were halfway across the main lobby where all the airlines have their ticket purchase counters. I was on a leash, which usually pisses me off, but I knew that Jimmy had to do it to make the public feel more comfortable about a big dog moving through a crowded area.

All of a sudden I picked up a whiff of an explosive detection marker. Whoa!! I put on the brakes. It jerked Jimmy to a stop. But he definitely likes to be the boss, especially in front of the public and definitely in a client's area. He commanded, "Heel!" and tried to walk. I knew my responsibility and I wasn't moving. Wake up, Jimmy, I thought. Get a clue here. This is not some arbitrary stubbornness. I was planted solid, so the leash pulled taut between us. He looked me straight in the eyes, an old, overused human alpha male trick. I stared back just as determined until he finally got the message.

He gathered the leash and sank on one knee next to me. "OK, boy." He unclipped the leash and whispered, "Find out what's going on here."

"Go!" About time, I thought. I took off running a large spiral as a way to home in on the smell. They use four different marker scents to enable detection of C-4 type plastic explosives like PETN, RDX or Semtex. Regardless, there is no mistaking the marker scent.

Some people on the concourse freaked out—they were not used to seeing a large dog homing in on a suspect in an airport lobby. I ran past a little kid who grabbed his mother's leg. "Mommy, mommy, the dog's gonna eat me!"

Jimmy rushed past the woman. "It's ok lady, he's working on a scent for me."

Of course, Jimmy takes all the credit. Oh well, it's a dog's life. I tracked the scent, getting stronger now. It was coming from baggage on a cart that belonged to two guys standing in the American Airlines ticket line. That's it! Time for aggression. I charged through the line of travelers and grabbed a tall blue bag in my teeth and started to shake it.

"Hey!" the guy yelled while he tried to kick me. "Get that God damned dog off my luggage!"

I snarled, "GRRRRRR!" It was the best I could do with my mouth full of luggage.

Jimmy had his iPhone out calling airport security. The guy who yelled was moving around getting in position to kick me. Shit, I thought, where's the cavalry when you need them.

We had accumulated an audience around us. I had let go of the dude's luggage, but I was still growling, threatening to eat his leg for dinner.

"Sir! Jimmy said, holding up his badge. "You better stand back and don't move. My dog is a trained killer. Kick him and you'll make his day."

Jimmy loves to quote Clint Eastwood lines like he's the San Francisco movie cop, Dirty Harry. He's not tall like Eastwood, but he's big, and he gets this look in his eye like a Hell's Angel who's just found some slimy dude on his motorcycle. The guy with the eager foot backed up and gave his partner a look that said, I don't like this. As Jimmy reached down to clip the leash on, three security guards arrived. They all looked like they were ready for action.

The guard in the middle said to eager foot, "Sir, you and your friend need to come with us and bring your luggage."

We all went off to a room in the security area where an inspector interrogated the two suspects and the guards started opening up the luggage. The luggage I was chewing on turned out to contain a golf bag with a full set of clubs. They checked it out and set it aside, "Nothin' in here but a bunch of golf balls."

I thought they'd be smarter, but what can you expect from humans? I went right over and grabbed the bag again, "Grrrrrrrrr."

One of the guards looked over, "What's the matter with your dog, man?"

Jim said, "There's something in there. You better check it out. He's grabbing the pocket with the golf balls."

They finally got the hint and an analysis of the golf balls determined that they were not golf balls at all, but a cleverly disguised plastic explosive, Semtex H which is fifty fifty, RDX (cyclotrimethylenetrinitramine) and PETN (pentaerythritol tetranitrate). Sorry, I like to show off a little knowledge once in a while.

But of course you know who got the credit for the bust, Mr. Alpha himself, my partner Jimmy. The American Airlines authorities were very happy that two terrorists-to-be did not get on one of their planes. In fact they were so happy, they told Jim he could go anywhere he wanted as a reward.

Jim said, "I've always wanted to go to Buenos Aires."

So, that's how I ended up a hero, stuck in a kennel for three weeks while Jimmy drank pina coladas in Buenos Aires.

Fear

When we kissed, I learned the meaning of the word fear. It was an emotion I did not expect, an emotion that began with that single touch and grew spontaneously from an archetypal knowledge lodged deep in my gut. It was nothing that I could express and nothing that I would ever relate to you. It could mean losing you and I could not suffer that loss now that we have found each other.

Love, especially a deep and lasting love has been a quest since the beginning of time—recounted in myriad stories and proclaimed in a million poems. The fact that I have stumbled onto such a love is beyond comprehension and it has thrilled me to my core. The sight of you creates a vibration inside me that overtakes reason and pushes me to the brink of madness. The touch of you creates such an intense reaction that I find it almost beyond the threshold of pain.

Just these thoughts alone engender a throbbing desire within me that I know must, at all cost be satisfied. I know that these ravings might seem outrageous to you, over the edge and irrational. I just can't help myself. I'm torn between divulging my feelings and taking the chance you would see me as the fool and baring my soul and forging between us an everlasting union that would be unparalleled.

Today is the day. Our courting was like an old-fashioned dance and it exacerbated my level of excitement to new levels. But today is the day to consummate our relationship—I know it, you know it. There is nothing in the way, no impediment, no family conflict, no competitor more suited than I am, nothing to prevent the fulfillment of our desires.

Mating is the ultimate communication. In this union, our two bodies will merge in a physical and emotional engagement. And now, even as these thoughts pour through me, we are moving together. It feels like magnetism, an irrevocable magnetism that I willingly give myself over to. I see your undulating movements and I feel myself respond in kind.

As we touch and couple together, our bodies vibrate in an exponential explosion of starburst magnitude. It is like flying; like soaring; like nothing I have ever experienced. It seems to go on and on and on with unbelievable rapture. And we finish, we complete—I am spent—I feel an immense calmness. Then, when you continue to touch me—it's a little aggressive, "Ouch!" I say, and the memory of that first fear rekindles—but I set it aside and luxuriate in my attraction to your eight gorgeous legs and the beautiful red hourglass on your abdomen. "Hey! Stop! That really hurts!"

Football

Paco's thin legs whirred like an electric mixer, beating the ground, and moving with the pack. He usually gained possession of the ball more than any other kid on his team.

Seven-year-old kids don't play strategy; they're a herd, focused, back and forth, toward one goal, and then, the opposite one.

Rafael watched his grandson and smiled. At seven years old, he already had a sense of the field, where the other players were, how they were moving and who was fast and who was slow. He had an instinct for moving the ball and unlike the other seven-year-olds on the team, he never, ever made the mistake of touching the ball with his hands. After all, this was football that the Americans called soccer. The name did avoid confusion with that "other" football.

This league for youngsters played two thirty-minute halves and this was the second. He enjoyed bringing Paco and he enjoyed watching the games. But today was hot, an Indian summer in late September, and he had forgotten his hat. A merciless sun beat down on him from a cloudless sky. Just sitting on his folding chair, he was sweating. He held a newspaper over his head to shade his eyes and protect himself.

Rafael guessed that the coach was close to calling off the game due to the heat.

For this age category, the coach had more than enough players. He kept ten plus a goalie on the field and rotated in the extras. However, Rafael noticed that Paco was on the field more than most of the others. The coach didn't play favorites, but he did like to win, and Paco was his best player. Rafael had the slightest twinge of guilt about the unfairness of that strategy, but he remembered how boring it was sitting on the bench before he, himself, was 'discovered'.

One of the boys on the other team kicked the ball down field toward his goal, but it was an air ball, flying up instead of toward the goal. A teammate ran under the falling ball to attempt a header, but he misjudged his position, and the ball hit the side of his head and shot out of bounds. The lineman blew his whistle and one of Paco's teammates ran out of bounds to get the ball and toss it in. Their coach yelled, "Positions, positions! Spread out!" The score was three to three and this might be the last chance for Paco's team to score and avoid a tie. Paco's teammate stood out of bounds, ball held over his head, two handed, as he feinted toward different receivers. The forwards, including Paco, jockeyed for an open position, but they were heavily guarded.

Suddenly, Rafael was dizzy. He sat on the sideline bench, but a dark cloud surrounded him with memories from his past. Reliving his game from years past, Rafael knew immediately that he had get the ball. Before he knew what was happening, Rafael's whole body froze, his arms and legs began to tingle. He struggled to recover, but the force of that game deja vu was overpowering. He blinked his eyes closed ... for just a second, as he attempted to regain his composure. Then he realized what had happened. Like a dream, he had been seeing his past football field, and why he reacted so strongly. It was a re-enactment of a similar scene that had occurred almost exactly thirty-five years ago, on that terrible day, the day of his personal calamity.

Mexico, his country, was hosting the International World Cup. They had reached the quarterfinals and Mexico was matched against a very strong Italian team. The date was burned in his memory, June 14, 1970.

Rafael was their best offensive forward, the favorite point man, the one player that Mexico's hopes were pinned on in this series of games watched by every country in the world. He had never felt better, never faster, never more capable than he did that day. Rafael had already scored during the first half for his team, and the Mexican crowd went wild ... a roar that he was certain could have been heard all over Mexico City. But then, Italy also scored, so they were tied.

Italy recovered the ball on a bad pass from the Mexican team and they kicked a long downfield pass. But, just like today, the receiver's header flew out of bounds, and it was Mexico's throw into play from the sidelines.

His teammate stood with the ball overhead, looking for a receiver, and again just like the scene today, his fullback broke into open territory and took the pass.

The searing sun's heat raised the air temperature on the arena field well into the eighties. The air sat like a hot wet blanket draping each player in a personal sauna. Rafael remembered the stands filled with people fanning themselves. It was like a mountain of butterfly wings. He wiped the sweat from his brow with his hand and it ran down onto his wrist. A drop escaped his hand, fell into his left eye and momentarily blinded him, a bad omen. He felt a second of panic but blinked and cleared his vision.

Like his grandson, Rafael also had an instinctive sense of the field, the players, the ball motion and what he should do. It was automatic, unthinking, and it had to be that way because there was no time for calculation or evaluation. He had to be in motion quickly enough to arrive at the receiving point for the pass he knew would be there.

His teammates knew he would be ready from the position of his arms, the movement of his legs and the slanted inclination of his body as he charged forward.

Rafael dodged his guard, just as he saw the ball rocket off the opposing fullback's foot. He was almost fifty yards from the goal as he received the pass and launched his own attack dribbling into scoring position. Straight ahead he saw the goal, the goalie and one defender. The crowd on both sides of the stadium was on its feet and the roar was deafening.

However, Rafael had lost track of two defenders, one gaining on him from behind and one from his right side. The Italians were fast. They converged in a pincer and just as Rafael cocked his right leg for a scoring shot, they slid toward the ball and into him so that both of their legs interlocked with his. Three forward motions tangled in a dynamic clinch that was impossible. The sound was like splitting wood, a cracking, an explosion of bone and flesh, an unearthly objection to the inconceivable.

All three men went down. Whistles blew. The two Italians extricated themselves and stood. Rafael, lying face down, pushed himself up on his elbows, then collapsed. His right leg below the knee was someplace it could never be. He would never play football again.

Mexico lost that game and Rafael watched from his hospital bed as Brazil went on to win the World Cup.

With his own game a vivid memory from years past, he knew immediately that he could have scored. The force of that loss was overpowering.

Now, today, once again in hospital, he realized he had been reliving his game against Italy on his grandson's football field and that's why he reacted so strongly.

Paco burst into the hospital ward yelling, "¡Abuelo! ¡Abuelo! ", as he rushed down the aisle.

Startled, Rafael replied, *"Qué?"*

"We won! My goal did it. We won!"

"Ay. Si. Muy bueno, nieto. Muy bueno."

Paco stopped. "Are you OK? You fell off the bench and we tried to lift you."

Rafael laughed and said, "Too much sun. I'm okay now that you are here."

Gamble

rrrrrrrrraaaaaarrrrrrrrraaaaaarrrrrraaaaaaarrrrrrrrr-
rrrrrrr!

The sound bounced off my garage walls. I twisted
the key off, "Just my luck!"

It was nine o'clock. I had already loaded my week's
work in the car, closed and locked the house and set
the alarm. It was a long drive to my rented room and I
needed a night's sleep before a tense Monday. I loved
living out in the country even if it meant a two-hour
commute to the South Bay every week. Tonight I had
delayed, to enjoy the evening coolness and the smell
of the creek.

Briefly, I considered calling AAA. No. I was not
going to hang on the phone and then wait a half-
hour or more for a tow truck. I could roll-start it. I
slipped the stick shift into neutral, released the hand
brake and stepped out of the car patting the roof like
you would a dog. My RX-7 sports car was my baby,
always clean and polished with a car cover for dust
free outside parking.

With my left hand on the steering wheel and my
right on the doorframe, I pulled the car backwards
and outside in a circle so it was in a flat spot at the top
of our long steep driveway. I reached in and pulled
the parking brake on and let the car door swing shut.

As I straightened up, the automatic garage light clicked off and I was in total darkness. An amplified wave of frog and cricket sounds surrounded me.

This was not the semi-darkness of city streets, or town roads lit by occasional house windows. This was deep closet blackness. I could not see my own hand.

Well, I thought, all I have to do is walk in front of the motion detectors and the driveway lights will pop on. "Rats!" They didn't come on because I had turned them off. Undecided for a moment about what to do, I reasoned that I could turn on the headlights as the engine started. So I got in and released the brake - but nothing happened. It was too flat.

No problem! I got out, gave the car a push and jumped back in as it started to roll. I couldn't see anything, but I knew what to do. I had roll-started cars on hills ever since high school. Clutch in, rolling fast downhill, I turned on the ignition, slipped into first gear and flipped on the lights. But I heard swish-swish - I had turned on the windshield wipers instead of the headlights - "NO!" In a panic, I jammed down on the brakes, pumped madly, but without the engine running, nothing happened!

Crrruuunnnccchhh! Scccreechhhh! Thump! Thump! Sssscccrraaaaaaaape! WUMP!

I sat, tilted sideways in the deep ditch on the left side of our driveway. Only the right headlight would come on, but I could see the small tree that stopped me and many, many bushes against the left side of my car. No one could hear me yell, "Stupid! Stupid! Stupid!"

Happy Hour

I strode into the lounge with the confidence of Jesus in my heart and a bible in my hand. Friday nights are the best times for these expeditions and tonight I had selected the Baja Cocktail Lounge on Stevens Creek Blvd near my temporary office in Silicon Valley. It was a sad round building with a South Sea ambiance worn thin by years of mediocre profits, multiple owners and no repairs. I went there straight from work so I could arrive before the noisy crowd.

It took me a few minutes to adjust to the dowdy lighting. Dusty fishnets draped the partitions and some of the walls. Crackled varnish surfaces leaked an invisible alcoholic vapor. There were no booths, just a bar and a dozen tables with three couples and a woman in a dark blue uniform sitting alone at a corner table.

I checked my appearance in the entrance mirror. Tall, with proud posture, thinning hair and rimless glasses. My subdued tie and gray slacks matched my navy blue sport coat. I could be any respectable businessman.

The woman at the corner table glanced up and I knew immediately that God wanted me to talk to her.

She watched me as I walked to her table and set the bible down so she could see the title. "Ma'am", I said, "If you would be so kind as to let me speak to you, I believe my message can help you."

I felt exposed, uncomfortable during the long pause waiting for her to answer, but then she said "Sit down." Her voice had a quiet and comfortable authority as though she owned this part of the building and could assign seats without fear of contradiction.

My voice croaked. I coughed. "Is it really all right?"

She locked eyes with me. "I wouldn't have said it if I didn't mean it. If we are going to talk, it should be as equals both at the same level. So, please sit down."

"Thank you," I said. "When I came into this room, I received a message from God that you were in need. I hope you don't think I'm presuming to be special. I'm just a messenger."

"Really?" she said.

Her voice made it a question. I was taken aback. She seemed so composed and I sensed no resistance, only curiosity. It was not the normal response I was used to, but I pressed on, "Do you believe in God?"

She said, "Yes. Do you?"

Her answer, another question, threw me off again. I felt just a twinge of defensiveness but I plunged ahead, "Absolutely. He gives me my life and He gives my life meaning. I only work to provide sustenance for myself so I can spread His word."

She tilted her head and brushed hair away from her eye as she asked, "What religious organization do you belong to?"

"I don't subscribe to an institutional religion. I work directly with the messages I receive from God."

"Hmm." Her eyebrows raised. "What regular job provides you sustenance?"

I paused. The conversation was beginning to sound strangely like I was being interviewed. If she was trying to rattle me, it wouldn't work. The word of the Lord was too strong in me. But it was important to be open and honest with her so I could introduce her to 'the Word', so I responded, "During the day, I'm a consulting accountant for Coopers and Lybrand."

"Ahh, so you are assigned to different companies on a contract basis."

"Yes. I am usually a member of a team. Most of the time I'm away from home."

"Where is home?"

"My parents live in Seattle. When I'm not assigned, I stay with them."

"Are your parents retired?"

She rebounds so quickly with questions, I need to turn this conversation back onto her, "No. Dad is a civil engineer for Bechtel and Mom is a minister. By the way, is that a Navy uniform you are wearing?"

"No. It's a Coast Guard uniform. I'm a lieutenant, junior grade, but you haven't told me your name?"

"John. Friends call me Jack."

"Well, Jack, some of my friends are due here in just a few minutes. I would like to talk to you, but I don't think this is the right place. Do you know Prospect Park?"

"Yes. It's not far from here."

"Right. I like to walk there in the afternoon on weekends. I'll meet you under the American flag in the center of the park at 1 PM tomorrow."

"OK." We shook hands and I left feeling strangely disoriented. I went to my apartment, but her image kept popping into my head. The exchange was so different from other religious encounters I had. That night, I fell asleep thinking about meeting her the next day.

~

By noon Saturday, the air was heavy with August heat. I decided to walk to the park. My work for Jesus was always exhilarating, but this time I felt an abnormal eagerness. I wanted to get to the park to see her again. As I walked, questions piled up. What was her name? Why did she arrange to meet me in the park? I suddenly realized that I was walking fast and my shirt, wet with sweat, was sticking to me.

I arrived 15 minutes early so I walked to the bench under the flagpole and sat down to wait. I wondered if she would come. I knew whatever happened, it was God's choice. I took out my bible to calm myself with the Word of the Lord. A few minutes after one, I saw her coming down the path. A sudden physical sensation overwhelmed me. Nothing like this had ever happened to me before. A fear grew in me that left me ice cold and trembling from head to foot. Jesus had left me. I jumped up and ran. I ran straight down the path and down the street and away from her. I ran until she couldn't see me. I ran until I was totally exhausted and could run no more.

A car horn shattered my temporary blindness. I was standing in the middle of the street. Embarrassed, I moved to the sidewalk and walked to the end of the block. The street sign read Blaney and Poinciana. I had only run four blocks, but I was ringing wet. I moved the bible to my left hand. It felt wet. I looked down at the dark imprint of my right hand on the cover. It was a reminder from God. 'Don't forget me', it said. The panic fell away and the day began to fall back into place. I must go back. The need to return loomed as all-important and I walked back.

As I entered the park I could see her on the bench under the flagpole, still there, waiting. She watched me walk toward her and said, "I had a hunch you'd return".

How could she know that? Transfixed for the moment, I realized she was not in uniform. Strange that I hadn't noticed it before. And her hair was different, down around her face, not pulled back in that severe way that pulled her ears tight and matched her uniform. She had silver earrings with an aqua colored stone that matched the color of the pattern on her slacks. Her white blouse had a soft round collar and cut off sleeves for the warm weather. She was slightly built, her blouse tucked into a narrow waist, her breasts pushed out against the buttons. I felt my blush coming before it happened and I rushed to speak to stop it, "God gave me a sign. It was the bible in my hand that let me know I had to return."

She smiled. It changed her, like theater sidelights that suddenly illuminated an actor's face. A warmth rose in my chest. I felt my own smile before it happened.

Confused, I sat next to her. Neither of us spoke. Park life continued like another world next to ours. A pre-teen wearing baggy pants with a T-shirt as long as a dress, rolled by on a skateboard scattering a dozen or so pigeons that were hoping for a handout. An Indian family had a picnic basket open on the grassy slope next to us. Their two children each had a rolled up piece of paras bread. Blackbirds high in the pines answered squeals from the children.

I said to her, "I don't know why I ran."

"You don't have to explain. I'm glad you came back."

Neither of us continued. The feeling was new to me and I grappled for the logic of it. It must be God moving in strange ways, but the need to be here felt very personal and not motivated by anything greater than my simple personal desires. Was I allowing my own selfish need to replace my mission? Was this sin? Why did it feel so natural and good to be here? A teenage boy and girl walked by, his arm around her waist, her hand in his back pocket.

Sitting next to me, she said, "Ruth."

My head snapped around. "What?"

She repeated, "My name is Ruth."

"Oh." Words would not come. It was stupid to say nothing but nothing came out.

She said, "Let's go for a walk."

We both stood and she took my hand. It had the impact of a lightning strike, every muscle tensed. Panic gathered again in my chest.

Ruth said, "Jack. It's OK."

"It's OK", I parroted.

We walked from the bench down a gravel path between flowering escallonia bushes. I glanced back in time to see a large opportunistic crow land on the back of the empty bench and hop down next to the Bible. It pecked the cover open, then ripped out a page and flew away with it.

Hills Like Brown Camels

(A Tribute to Ernest Hemingway)

Will drove west out of Nevada City. It was his day off and the kids were in school. Country Western music blared from the Sirius station. The blues vocals and guitar chords fit the mood of the late summer day. He fidgeted in his seat and glanced at his wife, wishing the lyrics would push everything out of his mind for the hour-long trip.

Sue stared out the passenger window of their pickup at the pines and scrub oaks on California's rolling brown hills. A few clouds floated above them like dabs of white frosting. The smell of degreasing soap on Will's hands from the morning's tune up on the truck lingered in the cab. Last night they had agreed to make this trip together. She brushed imaginary crumbs off her jeans. "You'll be okay."

"I know," he said.

She turned the radio down. "You know you're driving a little fast."

"There's no traffic."

"Still . . ." she said.

"Don't nag me, Sue Ann. It's not a good day for it."

"You don't have to snap."

"I didn't snap, I just asked you not to nag me."

"It wasn't what you said, it was how you said it."

His voice puffed up. "I don't wanna argue."

"I just wanted you to know about your tone of voice.

"I said, I don't wanna argue."

After a pause, she said, "You're nervous, aren't you."

"No, I'm not."

"It's normal to be a little nervous."

"I'm not nervous."

She looked out the side window again. "Okay. You're not nervous."

He slowed as they drove through the town of Rough and Ready. A rusted flat bed truck and a car were parked in front of the one store. A boy in baggy pants and a baseball hat turned backwards, stood in front holding his bike. When they passed the town, Will sped up and the tires squealed on the first turn.

She said, "We've plenty of time. There's no hurry." He didn't answer, but she noticed his frown.

He said, "Can you reach that bottle of water in the back seat?"

"Sure, honey." Sue twisted around, grabbed the bottle, and handed it to him.

He drank and handed it back to her as he slowed for a farm tractor. She rolled down her window.

He said, "Why'd you do that?"

"What?"

"Roll down your window."

"I wanted to smell the warm summer air and the trees."

"Makes too much noise."

She hesitated like she was going to say something, but then rolled the window up.

The farm tractor turned off and he sped up again. They listened to Tim McGraw singing *Live Like You Were Dying*. When it finished, she said, "That's one of my favorites."

Will nodded. "Mine, too."

She said, "We've got a lot in common."

He shifted in his seat and checked the mirrors. "Yeah."

"Do you really think we have a lot in common or are you just saying that?"

"Why don't you believe me when I say things? I already said we did."

Almost too softly for him to hear, she said, "I just wanted to know for sure."

"It's for sure. We have lots in common. We always have. Are you satisfied?"

"You don't have to get surly." She couldn't help the resentment in her voice.

"I'm not surly, God damn it, I'm just trying to figure out why you're asking me all these questions today."

She waited until they passed a bumpy part of the road so that the toolbox mounted on the back of the pickup stopped rattling, then said, "Other people have had this done."

"So?"

"I mean, it's not very serious."

He flashed back, "It's serious to me. I won't be the same." He paused. "What makes you think it ain't serious?"

"They said it was just a small cut."

"Sure, small to you. You're not getting cut."

"You know what I mean. It's not like having a baby."

He slowed down for the right turn onto highway 20 to Marysville, stopped and waited for several cars to pass. He glanced at her, then back at the road and said, "I suppose."

"What?" she said.

"I suppose I know what you mean about," he rubbed the back of his neck, "getting cut."

She saw him wince at the word 'cut.' After a few minutes they passed the Penn Valley intersection and she said, "It won't make a difference . . . you know, between us."

"Oh?" he said. What if it does . . . make a difference?"

"It won't."

"Easy for you to say."

"They said it wouldn't make a difference. We asked. And I'll still care for you just as much, honey."

"Sure," he said, sarcasm twisting the sound of his voice, "but there's a part of me you won't be able to care for any more." He slowed for a car making a turn, then sped up, and said, "I just don't like the idea of it." Before she could say anything, he reached over and turned the radio up to hear Joe Nichols sing *Tequila Makes Her Clothes Fall Off.*

As soon as the song finished, she turned off the radio.

He said, "What'd you do that for?"

"So we can talk."

"I don't want to talk."

"I think we should talk. You're doing this for both of us and you just said you don't like the idea of it. "

"Okay, you talk. I don't have a thing to say." He looked straight ahead at the road, both hands on the steering wheel, while the pickup engine hummed like a hundred busy bees and the silence sat between them like a tall gray wall.

They passed the turnoff to Brownsville and she said, "You never told me that you didn't like the idea of it."

"Well," he said, "I don't."

"I thought we decided it was easier for you to do than for me, and it cost less."

He said, "Yeah . . . we did."

Down in the flat lands, they were passing occasional ranch homes. Tree lined ravines divided the land and turkey vultures circled overhead. She rested her head against the window. "The hills look like brown camels."

"Camels?" he laughed and reached down and turned the radio on in time to hear the end of *Strawberry Wine*.

She said, "That's Deana Carter singing."

"I know."

"You didn't have to laugh when I said the hills looked like brown camels."

"Sorry. It slipped out. Didn't mean nothin'."

"Are you changing your mind?"

"What?" he said, his tone incredulous.

She repeated slowly, "Are you changing your mind?"

"I didn't say anything about changing my mind."

"I know, but you said you didn't like the idea of it."

"I don't like the idea of a lot of things: muckin' out the barn, fixin' the septic system, repairin' the damn truck, castrating', but I still do 'em. We have to do a lot of things that we don't like the idea of and I don't change my mind about them."

Inside the city limits of Marysville, they worked their way through several intersections of traffic lights, then drove the bridge over the river into Yuba City.

She continued, "This isn't like a chore."

"I know it isn't."

"You don't have to do it."

"I know."

"Have you thought about not doing it?"

He pulled into the Medical Center lot and parked in a space, turned to her and said, "Of course, I've thought about not doin' it." He turned the key, the engine died, and the music stopped.

Judgment Day

There was little time before Dmitri arrived. Brian, Michael and Clark hurried into their leotards and tights while standing in the crowded restroom, a small space with a toilet stall, a urinal and a short bench along one wall. One dusty, cobwebbed window leaned open above them, but it didn't dispel the annoying smell of urine that lingered around each worn green painted surface. The normal arrhythmic buzz of cars rushing by on the city street outside created an intimidating pressure in the air. Brian struggled to pull his tights over clammy skin. He wrenched them to his waist. Anxious shoulder muscles taut, he clipped on an elastic belt. Today he would be compared and valued, then bought or passed over; a commodity. His first qualm.

Dmitri Petrovitch and his wife, Yelen, ran this school for classical Russian ballet. Dmitri had the subservient respect of principal dancers from famous ballet companies around the world. Whatever he did to deserve this would never be questioned by anyone in this studio. He seldom talked to anyone in his classes either when he arrived or when he left. He existed somewhere beyond normal conversation. Brian frequently stayed to watch him conduct the advanced class. Dimtri didn't smile and he never gave approval, only disapproval. The highest form of praise in his class was to complete the one and a half hours without criticism. Brian respected and feared him.

Balancing on one leg at a time, Brian pulled leg warmers over his calves and slipped on both ballet slippers. He straightened, "Well." he said, "I'm as ready as I'll ever be." His voice sounded cocky and more confident than he felt. Michael ignored him with an impassive smile that irritated Brian. At 17, Michael had advanced to the intermediate class after only two years of beginning ballet. Brian, ten years older, had watched Michael conquer the leaping jete' en tournant with no effort, a step it took Brian weeks to learn. Michael would probably move up today; an achievement that Brian desperately wanted. Acceptance into Dmitri's advanced class was the ultimate approval, his Mount Everest.

Clark responded, "Kick ass, man! You can make it. Don't let the old son-of-a-bitch give you the evil eye. You've really improved this year. I'm sure he'll pick you for advanced. It's just like my real estate business. I kept the pressure on and made it. I just kept picking up foreclosures and flipping them...."

Brian interrupted, " Not now, Clark."

"Ok. Ok. I like to talk. It's my business you know."

Brian said, "I know that," as he slipped out the door.

Yelena claimed she could teach anyone to dance in her beginning and intermediate classes. Clark was her challenge. He was 40-ish, about 6 feet tall, muscular and clumsy. She finally moved him to intermediate after five years in the beginning class.

Brian remembered when he started ballet on a dare. Now he needed this daily intermediate class like a drug habit. It made him feel different, although, unlike a drug, it was a positive addiction.

Outside he was ordinary, divorced, dating and a computer techie like most everyone he knew in Silicon Valley. As a dancer he felt special, elevated. At first he was flattered by the attention he drew particularly from women when he introduced himself as a dancer. Then, as he improved, ballet consumed him, mind and body, like a religion. Moving with music for Brian had become spiritual. He identified ballet with his soul. Ballet was who he was.

Brian and Michael left the change room and entered the studio. Both were lean, about the same height, 5'10", Michael had dark hair, dark eyes with white skin and fine Northeastern European features; Brian had reddish brown hair, hazel eyes with some freckles and fair skin typical of an Irish complexion.

The dance space they entered was unusually wide and deep with a two-story ceiling and huge mirrors across the entire front that glistened with relentless copies of everything in the real room. An old upright piano was pushed against the left wall. The entrance vestibule and the change room they had just left, were on the right.

For a long time, the mirrors had intimidated Brian. Frivolous primping was looked down on with disdain in the matter of fact culture of his Irish Catholic family. Mirrors were associated with silly young girls. Men had no time for staring at themselves and boys could care less what they looked like. But mirrors in a dance studio provided immediate and necessary feedback on posture and position in order to make corrections, so Brian reconciled his cultural aversion.

The class buzz was gone today, replaced by tension. Faces around the room were tight. Dmitri visited Yelena's intermediate class once a year to determine who would move up to his advanced class. Advanced was a demanding hour and a half daily performance under a microscope more critical and more incisive than any surgeon's knife. And Dmitri was not kind. There was only one correct way, his Russian way. Yet everyone, including Brian wanted an invitation into his class.

Brian turned to Michael, "Let's get the barre."

Normally the permanent barres on the walls were enough, but two portable barres were kept in the studio for large classes. As usual, Michael followed Brian without answering. They each took the ends of a barre one at a time and carried them to the center of the room. They took positions on the opposing sides of one of the portable barres. Girls were filing out of their larger changing room and taking positions around the room, a few with Michael and Brian in the center.

Brian closed his eyes to focus on his body. Muscles he was not usually aware of were taut. Time, he thought, for stretching. He did a few plie's, in first, heels together, second, wide to the side and the inhumane fifth, feet opposing and together. He reached for his feet in fifth. Too stiff. He had to loosen up. He did some bends to the side and then, with both hands on the bar, leaned over with a flat back and straight legs to stretch the muscles he knew would give him trouble in his lower back.

Brian watched as Clark walked out of the dressing room and took a position at the barre in a far corner of the room. There was no chance for him to advance and he was exposing himself to ridicule. Brian wondered why he decided to come to this class and he felt a brief pinch of sympathy. Maybe Clark also had an invisible mountain to climb.

Brian looked around. Everyone was present. Walking in late to any class that Dmitri taught was asking for trouble.

Time expanded for Brian. He noticed details for the first time that had always been there; the faded green paint on the walls, the musty overhead fluorescents and the hint of healthy odor of locker room sweat mixed with the flowery scent of teen girl's perfume.

No one talked above a whisper and most of the dancers were stretching. Michael in white leotard and white tights continued through his basic stretches oblivious of the many eyes on him. He was not unusually muscled, but there was something animal about his motions, something cat-like, which attracted attention. Brian found himself following Michael's hands as they moved through the air.

Sound in the room stopped. Brian turned toward the entrance where Dmitri had begun his strange atrophied shuffle to the single chair that sat in the center of the room in front of the mirrors. Rain or shine, heat or cold, he wore an old faded sport jacket and a shawl. He carried the walking stick that he used for every class. It had an ivory head and Yelena had told Brian that Serge Diaghilev had given it to Dmitri when he and Yelena left the Ballet Russe of Monte Carlo and traveled to the United States.

He reached his chair, leaned his stick against the mirror, draped his coat on the back and unwound his shawl laying it over the arm. He inspected the class with small critical eyes. He may have been over 5 feet when he danced, but he had shrunk with age. Taller, he could be typecast as Scrooge. No one moved.

Dmitri sat in his chair, center stage, facing the class, with his walking stick in his right hand, just like Moses ready to create a path. But Dmitri had no interest in the sea. He was there to part the strong from the weak, the winners from the losers, and the advanced from the intermediate. It was the day for judgment.

He looked to his right at the empty piano bench. His eyebrows drew down and together. Red crept across his face like successive applications of rouge. He turned toward the open doorway to the vestibule on his left. "Yelena!"

No one breathed.

He repeated, "YELENA! WHERE IS THE PIANIST?"

Danny Lawrence scurried across the room behind the dancers, sat at the piano and tried to look like he wasn't late. Long ago he had memorized every piece of music they needed. He knew what to play for every dance combination that the Petrovichs taught.

Yelena walked in. There was a simultaneous and almost inaudible sigh of relief. She, not Dmitri, was going to lead the exercise.

"All right students, first position, stand up straight. Mr. Petrovitch wants to see only straight backs. Maria! Put your fingers together. You know better than that. Everyone ready now? ..... Cara. Eyes straight ahead. Mr. Lawrence."

It was her command for music. Danny immediately began Korsakov's Capriccio Espanol.

Brian liked Yelena. Maybe it was because she paid him special attention. However, he thought it was primarily because there were so few men interested in dance. Once, she had taken him aside to show him a photograph of Dmitri and herself dancing the tango in a nightclub during the depression. It was a normal thing to do, but for Yelena it was clandestine. She revealed the photo as though it was their secret, Brian's and hers.

Yelena arrived at the studio every day with a hat and gloves on. She always wore dresses that were pale and Midwestern, like Dorothy's aunt Em in the Wizard of Oz. She was slight and frail in appearance, but had the legs of a dancer. Teaching class she would demonstrate steps wearing medium heel black shoes, flowing across the floor with secret strength. It always surprised Brian. Today she would not teach, but only direct the class for barre and center floor. Everyone knew that Dmitri would direct the more difficult moving dance combinations.

Yelena called out each move, demi-plié, grand plié, relevés, and port de bras. Next, came the battement moves to limber the legs and feet, then the rond de jambe, more sweeping leg moves and finally several different pirouettes at the bar, dehors and dedans, i.e. outside and inside turns.

Brian did the initial barre work like a mantra. His body desired the moves and it took over. It was comfortable, known and relaxing. But as soon as rond de jambe was called, Brian began to reach. He consciously sent commands to each muscle, 'be perfect, and be straight', while he integrated his motion with Melody in F from the piano.

After barre pirouettes, Yelena was ready to move on. "Put the barres away please."

Brian and Michael each grabbed an end of their barre and walked it off the floor. Clark walked up behind them carrying the second barre by himself, muscles bulging with the effort.

As he passed them he said, "Piece a' cake, gents."

Yelena circulated through the room placing dancers by ability, the best in the front row, newer students in the second row. She directed, "You boys spread out behind the girls. Make a third row." It was a tradition, girls in the front for beauty, boys in back for strength.

In the center floor without a barre, adagio movements emphasized balance. Brian was now completely focused. His entire body was warm, fears pushed into a small closet in his mind.

Yelena worked the girls through posture positions, including arabesques and attitudes, and then simple soutenu turns. Dimiri was watching. She progressed into allegro movements and battements. Lawrence, on the piano, switched to Polonaise Militaire. Yelena asked for battement développé, then relevés, followed by échappé, and changement de pied.

One part of Brian queued his muscle memory, kept time to the music and commanded perfect moves. The other watched the girls en pointe, amazed at their ability wearing impossible toe shoes. To be considered for advanced work they had to do everything en pointe. This was the girl's show.

Yelena stopped for a moment, "It's time for pirouettes, girls. Remember a line straight through the top of your head. Be tall."

It was her first hint at teaching, a reminder that any slouching would make you fall off your pirouette.

Brian breezed through single and double pirouettes from several positions. He was absorbed in his effort, ignoring the girls, until.........

Bang! Bang! Bang! Dimtri's walking stick pounded the floor. Yelena turned.

Dmitri pointed his stick at a girl in the front row, "Back."

She shrank back to the second row, eyes tear-glistened. She would stay intermediate.

Yelena took advantage of the interruption, "Now for the air turns boys, a single l'air tour."

Danny began the Hungarian Dance on the piano. The girls moved back and Michael, Brian and Clark moved to the front.

Brian felt charged, nerves, muscles, fibers held tight, vibrating, ready to move.

Yelena called them by name, "Michael".

Michael extended his right foot into a perfect tendu, slid it quickly back into a tight fifth position plié, and leaped straight up into a full turn, landing in a perfect fifth plié.

"Brian."

Brian, now fully focused on his body, moved his foot to a tendu and his arms to second. He pulled in his right foot to fifth plié and right arm to first and launched straight up. Like time travel, he was suddenly back in fifth plié with no memory of the transition. He glanced at Yelena and saw a slight smile. Dmitri was watching him. It had been a good air turn. He had a surge of excitement. He wanted more. He wanted to do it again, to wrap ballet around him like a shield.

"Clark."

Brian could see Yelena's lips draw tight. Clark was a burden. He prepared, did his plié, and leaped into a turn only to fall back at an angle and stumble to his left. Dmitri shook his head.

"All right Michael, a double air turn, please."

Yelena rarely used English, but she wanted to make sure there were no mistakes today.

Brian watched Michael, incredulous as he prepared for the leap with an expression of disinterest. He sank into his plié, leaped into two complete turns and landed in a perfect fifth position plié. Dmitri nodded his recognition and looked next at Brian.

Unnecessarily, she called his name, "Brian."

Brian felt strong, but Michael's nonchalant perfection shook him. An icy twinge raced up his back. Automatically suppressing it, he prepared, pulled into a good fifth plié and leaped. Again he was back in plié on the other side of the time warp, and he had completed two good turns in the air, but he was slightly off balance. He quickly corrected his balance with his arm but Dmitri saw it. He didn't miss a thing, damn him.

She called out, "Clark."

Clark just shook his head. Center floor work was finished for him.

Yelena announced, "Class. Mr. Petrovitch will lead the dance combinations. Please begin with chaînés diagonally from the back left corner of the room; when you finish, start from the right. Girls first, front row only, then the boys." She paused, "Second row, you are dismissed."

Chaînés turns were easy, spinning on half-toe in a straight line, but it required proprioception as those dancers that finished went to the opposite rear corner and started across diagonally threading through the spaces in the first line.

Dmitri watched for a while, then clapped his hands to stop the step and motioned to Anne, the best intermediate dancer with his stick. She moved out and he demonstrated the first dance step with his hands. It was a bizarre way to communicate. Dmitri rarely got out of his chair and even more rarely did a step himself.

Anne finally understood and did a glissade, glissade, pas de chat, assemblé. It was a simple sequence from fifth position, slide, slide, and a little cat leap then a small hop assembling her feet back into fifth.

Dmitri said, "Girls only."

Brian watched the girls as they started across the room one at a time, hard-toed pointe slippers thump-thumping against the floor. His own arms and legs made small mimic motions in time to the music in virtual practice. Involuntarily, he began to hum. He felt like an Indy-car racing its engine; eager for the track.

Bang! Bang! Dmitri stopped the step with his stick. He pointed at the girl in front of him, "Fifth!"

She snapped the offending foot tight against the other, eyes wide and biting her lip to keep from crying.

Dmitri motioned to the lead dancer, Anne again. He took her through the same step and added a pirouette at the end. She demonstrated once, and then returned to her place in line.

"Music!"

The line continued.

Bang! Bang! Dmitri stopped at the same girl. He pointed his stick at her, "You dance like a houseboat! Out!"

She ran from the studio, sobbing.

Yelena standing in the doorway announced, "That's all for today, girls. You can change. It's time for the men."

Dmitri motioned Michael out to do the demonstration. It was the same combination the girls did, but for the men he replaced the pirouette en l'air tour.

"Music!"

Danny began music from Swan Lake.

Michael stepped up. Tendu, then he took off across the room, his moves feline and every position perfect in time to the music.

Brian watched Michael's every muscle, every move through each repetition across the floor. The air turn mixed with moving steps made this combination difficult. He knew that Dmitri had done this on purpose to differentiate them. As soon as Michael finished, Brian posed. Charged up, he stood so straight he could feel his abdomen muscles stretch. The introduction finished and he flew on the first note of the melody.

Brian had out-of-body mental images of himself moving. Gravity didn't exist, only his body in flight existed. He arrived in his first fifth plié, cocked for the air turn and soared straight up and around. He landed balanced and flew into the next glissade. He smiled to himself at his success as he landed balanced again.

Bang! Bang! Bang!

Brian jerked back to the real world, frozen in place directly in front of Dimtri, like a butterfly stuck on a pin. Dmitri's walking stick was pointed at his feet. He looked down.

Dmitri commanded, "Fifth!"

His feet were several inches apart, more fourth than fifth. Too late, he corrected.

"Music," Dmitri ordered.

Danny played and Brian did one more combination. He leaned into his air turn and landed off balance.

Dmitri stood, gathered his things and prepared to leave.

Brian was dismissed. Discouraged, he looked around the room. Michael and Clark had disappeared. He walked off the floor to the change room.

After changing into street clothes, Brian started toward the front exit with his bag over his shoulder.

Yelena standing near the door took a step and touched his arm, "Brian."

He smiled at her, "I know. Next year, work on fifth position."

Proclivity

S am Campbell sat in the waiting room, definitely
feeling uncomfortable. He was a little early for his
four o'clock appointment. The shipping and receiving
department of Stacey's Bookstore where he worked
closed at three, and it only took him fifteen minutes to
walk up the street to this office. It was easier to walk
in downtown San Francisco than to drive.

There were a variety of things to read: People,
Cosmopolitan, several travel magazines and quite a
few issues of Psychology Today. He thought that was
probably normal for a shrink's office, but he really
didn't know, since he had never in his life visited one
of these guys.

Sam didn't read any of the magazines. He was
too nervous. He just looked around at the room and
fidgeted in his chair. The overhead fluorescents were
turned off and the light in the room came from a floor
lamp and a table lamp. It was definitely subdued but
it didn't seem to help him. The ceiling was white, but
the walls were a very light green color and all the furniture was nondescript beige. He was glad that no
one else was there.

The entrance door was stenciled with the name,
Dr. Raymond Striker, Psychologist, and the door
between the waiting room and the shrink's office was

blank. He could hear murmurs of a conversation but he couldn't make out any words, no matter how hard he listened. That was reassuring.

He thought, nuts! This is crazy. I don't want to talk to this guy. I'm only doing it for Sally and for all I know, this guy's a kook. I got enough trouble with work and Sally and bills to pay that I don't need some head knocker foolin' around with my brain.

Sam stood and started toward the outside door. Just then the inside door opened and he heard a woman say, "Goodbye Doctor. I'll see you next week." Sam turned toward an abstract watercolor hanging on the wall, held one hand up to partially cover his face and pretended to be studying the painting. After the woman left, he heard a male voice, "You must be Mr. Campbell. Please come in."

Shit, he thought, I almost made it out the door. Well … I may as well go through with it.

Sam turned to see a tall man, graying hair, past middle age, but not old. He had an athletic posture that was accentuated by his muscled arms, sport clothes, tan and tuft of chest hair visible where his shirt wasn't buttoned. He held the door for Sam and closed it behind him.

"Please sit down Mr. Campbell." He motioned to an overstuffed chair opposite his and as he sat down he picked up a pad and a pen that were on the small table next to his chair. He continued, "I normally record conversations, but I only do that with my client's permission and since this is our first meeting I'll just make a few notes to jog my memory if that's alright with you."

"Sure." Sam became aware that there was a window, but the blind was closed.

The doctor then asked Sam several routine questions about his work, marriage, activities and early family life. Sam began to relax a little.

Then the doctor stopped, looked at Sam for a minute and said, "All right, now it's your turn."

"Whadda ya mean my turn?"

"Your turn to talk."

"I don't wanna talk." Sam glanced at the door to make sure he knew where it was.

"Didn't you come here to discuss something with me?"

Sam stiffened up, looked around the room, then said, "Well, sort of."

"You have to talk to me Mr. Campbell. I can't help you if you don't talk to me."

"Look! You're a shrink. I don't really go for shrinks. You guys jus' charge big bucks for a lotta talk that I can get at the bar with the guys."

Sam noticed a slight peeve cross the other man's face as he said, "Shrink is slang! I'm a doctor, Mr. Campbell."

This just irritated Sam. "Jesus Christ, will you stop with the Mr. Campbell stuff. My name is Sam. Just call me Sam and I'll call you doc! How about it?"

There was a blue tension in the room and neither man spoke. The doctor stared at Sam and Sam began to wonder why in God's name he was paying for this.

Finally the doctor said, "You must have had something on your mind when you made the appointment, Mr., ahhh, …Sam."

"Yeah, my wife, Sally, said I had to come."

"You didn't want to come?"

"Right! I didn't want to come."

"Why did you?"

"Shit, I dunno. Curious, I guess. An' she kept buggin' me."

"What was she bugging you about … Sam?"

Sam clammed up. He thought, Oh shit, now I've done it. I didn't really want to talk about this and I had to open my big fat mouth. God dammit anyway. He looked down at the floor and fervently wished he were somewhere else.

The doctor continued, "You want to tell me about it, Sam?"

Sam struggled for a few minutes then said, "Okay, doc. It's something I wear and she thinks it's weird."

Sam doesn't continue, so there's a long silence. Finally the doctor says, "Yes, and?"

Sam still looked at the floor and said in a small voice, "It's a wig."

"Oh, a toupee."

"No."

"No?"

"No," Sam continued in a very small voice, "it's a chest wig."

"Oh."

Sam said, "I know it's weird, jus' like she said."

The doctor said, "I wear one."

Sam's head popped up and his mouth dropped open.

The doctor unbuttoned another top shirt button and said, "See."

Sam said, "I'll be Goddamned."

The two men stare at each other for a long time. Then the doctor said, "Where did you get yours?"

Spelling Bee

The overhead lights were hot, two television cameras were pointed at him and he could feel the sweat on the inside of his shirt. This was the annual 2020 runoff for the school 8th grade spelling bee sponsored by television station KNAK. Ray and Sara were the only two contestants left of the ten who had reached this level.

He liked Sara. They were friends and Sara had challenged him to enter the contest at his 13th birthday party last month. He remembered the party, the kiss, the touch of her hair while they slow-danced. Glancing at her next to him woke feelings that buzzed through his body. Now they were in competition with each other and the winner would travel to the Capitol for the State's annual spelling bee grand finale. He wanted to win, but he would probably lose her as a friend. Should he lose on purpose? It would be dishonest. He was angry at himself for even considering it.

Mr. Breckinridge, their high school principal, was conducting this bee. He looked up and said, "Sara, your word is, exacerbate. It's a transitive verb that means to make more violent or bitter, to cause to become more severe."

The cameras shifted focus to Sara. Ray noticed that her forehead creased ever so slightly and he knew she was struggling with the word. He silently wished her to get it right. She asked, "Can you use it in a sentence, please?"

"Yes. The threat of terrorism will exacerbate tension."

A small audience of family and a few friends sat stiff and straight. Their whispers stopped. Sara began, "Exacerbate, E-X ... A ... S-E-R ... B-A-T-E, exacerbate."

As soon as she finished, she knew from the look on Mr. Breckinridge's face that her answer was wrong. Her eyes dropped. Ray twinged. Her failure hurt him.

"I'm sorry, Sara. The correct spelling is E-X-A-C-E-R-B-A-T-E, exacerbate."

But Sara was only eliminated if Ray spelled the next word correctly. If they both missed, they would each have another word to spell. Breckinridge spoke, "Your word, Ray, is belletrist. It means one who creates literature of aesthetic value, rather than informative."

The quiet was startling. No one moved, not the television crews, the producers, the soundmen, the audience or Sara. Ray hesitated. He didn't want to beat Sara. If he wins, would she ever forgive him? He felt the audience's eyes and the eyes of everyone at home with a television set, watching him. The air smelled like hot electric insulation. It was thick, hard for him to breathe. He was afraid to look at Sara.

Ray had never heard of this word and he could only guess at its spelling from its sound. He took out a tissue, wiped his forehead, and then said the work out loud, "belletrist." The word didn't even sound right to him. He thought about another word, bellicose. It had an "i" after the double "l." But it was from the Latin, bellum, that meant war. That didn't seem right. He remembered that the belle of the ball was a pretty girl, probably from the French. That word had an "e" after the double "l." He continued, "B-E-L-L," then he stopped. "e" or "i" He gambled, "E ... T-R-I-S-T, belletrist."

Breckinridge paused and Ray held his breath. Then he saw the slight tilt of his head ... as Breckinridge said, "Correct!"

Ray closed his eyes for a moment; let the tension drain out. Now Sara was eliminated. He really cared for her more than he cared about winning the contest. He looked across the stage where they both stood at their microphones. Sara's face blossomed into the warmest most beautiful smile he had ever seen and Ray answered with his own smile.

Surprise

A stage hand finishes mopping the black Marlee dance floor as I stand in the wings, with the other male dancers, stage right, next to the sidelights. Nervously awaiting my queue, I mash more resin under the soles of my ballet shoes.

The set from the previous number has been moved backstage, and the curtain is closed. The overhead work lights go off and the pipe lights with the colored Fresnel lenses come on dim.

I still don't know why I agreed to do this. Maybe because I *do* like Claude Bolling's music and his piece, 'Romance,' is particularly sensual, or maybe I just succumbed to the choreographer's exuberance about her work, or maybe it was my own ego. Really, I'd just like to be at home reading a good mystery, but here I am. I pull each leg behind me to stretch my quads.

My partner stands in the wings on the opposite side of the stage with the other women dancers. Eight of us are arranged as four couples. I can hear the audience through the curtain, a dull wave of white noise. This dance should be easy, I tell myself, just like one more rehearsal. And we've rehearsed this at least a hundred times. Yet my heart pounds like it wants to jump out of my chest. I tell myself to calm down. The dance is only six minutes long. It'll be over before I know it. It's hot under the lights and my leotard already sticks to me. I see the other dancers move into their positions. Thank God I start in the back row, although I do have to move up onto the front apron several times. I try reason. What can go wrong? None of the steps are very hard. It's just a short combination, like a ballet class exercise, only with an audience. I wonder how many people are out there. I know some of my friends are coming and my girlfriend promised to come ... to give me moral support, she said. Why did I let her come? She'll see me make a fool of myself. I stretch again to relieve my tension. It'll be okay, I tell myself. Sure it will. It's just another dance step to music that I like.

I rehearse the steps in my head. Count four measures, the first two couples in front move out, then on the fifth measure I move toward my partner. We all meet in the center, in a quadrangle, then *balance'* left, *balance'* right, turn toward our partners, circle in an improvised waltz step, then I pose to support my partner in a pirouette, and ... The coach taps me on the shoulder and whispers, "Ready?"

I nod, but I don't feel ready. I feel disconnected from everything, disconnected from my body. The pulleys creak as the curtain slides back. I hear a cough. Two coughs. At least two people are out there.

The house lights are off, the audience is a dark void. I can't see a thing. The quiet behind me backstage is like a heavy weight. I feel dampness under my arms.

The music starts and after one measure the overhead Fresnel comes up and the footlights come on. I count four measures and the first two couples run out, then slide in a glissade toward each other. Measure five and I start.

I move toward my partner, my every body movement automatic, eyes locked with hers, permanent stage smiles fixed on our countenances. I say to myself, don't think. Let it be reflex, but keep counting. The *balance'* sequence is done and we start in the first full circle around the stage, a sort of jazz dance promenade. Everything is working. It feels right. Memories of coaching directions fill my head: Be graceful. Present yourself proudly, move smoothly, arms arching, fingers together, painting the air like a great work of art, feel the music.

The second time circling around the stage, I'm in front on the apron. I turn backwards, ready to support my partner's simple pirouette, I take four quick steps to get behind her, but she has missed her queue! Where is she?

I freeze for a quarter note—panic floods through me—I listen to the music—the show must go on. We need two—no, five measures to recover. The other dancers freeze—they see my problem. A combination pops into my mind from ballet class—it's sixteen counts—perfect. It will give everyone four measures to resume their partner positions and a measure to finish the dance.

I take a small leap sideways, a *pas de chat* then *assemble'* to get my right foot in front in fifth position *plie'*, one measure done. The other dancers are using the time to *balance'* into their final positions. Next I leap straight up four times, beating my calves, *entrechat*; two more measures done. Finally for the next measure I do a simple *battement tendu* and move my right foot to second position like I'm preparing for a pirouette, but instead I close in fifth *plie'* and launch into a double *l'air tour*, two leaping full turns. That's the last measure and now everyone is back in place. I reach around my partner's waist and we finish as choreographed.

The applause is unexpected, enthusiastic—we get two curtain calls before the final curtain is pulled closed. I stand there, unable to move, an empty scarecrow, shocked at what I did.

The work lights come up. An amplified voice says, "Clear the stage please."

My girlfriend is standing in the wings holding a small red rose. I move toward her.

She says, "You were really good. You deserve this. I didn't know you had a solo part."

The choreographer, standing behind her, gives me a knowing wink, smiles and nods her head.

"Well," I say "… it was kind of a surprise."

The Decision

Jason had worked himself out of a job. The more he thought about it the more uncomfortable he got about the decision he had to make. He zipped up his jacket and held one hand over his glasses to fend off the foggy drizzle as he walked through the coal mine parking lot darkness to his car, the last one in the AquaTech Corporation lot. Once again, he had stayed late, this time to personally test the final prototype of his underwater wrist computer for divers before its first public demo the next morning.

A twist of the key and his little old VW bug started up. Funny. The techies drove old clunkers while the secretary pulled up every morning in a Mercedes. He switched on the windshield wipers as he started out of the lot and glanced at his dashboard clock, surprised that it was already past midnight. This project, his project, had had a great run, but now, the decision he had promised to make tomorrow, loomed before him like Dickens' ghost of Christmas future.

The idea for his wristwatch product had popped into his head during a vacation in the Caribbean. For two years, he had led the project design team and tomorrow's demo meant its completion. He smiled to himself. This product was going to wow customers. And for his future, Jason had already been courted by two competing design groups inside the company, a hardware project led by his friend, Sam, and a software project led by Moira. He should be happy about that, but the pressure made him anxious.

He pulled onto Freeway 85 wondering if the other drivers buzzing past him were overachievers like himself or just shift workers just going to work. Regardless, his adrenalin peaked. One of those big GMC behemoths could crush his little bug and him in it. He pushed his old VW bug up to its top speed, 65 mph, and stayed in the slow lane, listening to the hypnotic plunk-plunk of the tires on the concrete roadway and watching defensively in his rear view mirrors.

Sam Chatterjee had approached him almost a year ago about joining his high tech design group at Aquatech. Jason knew they were into concept development and it sounded really interesting, but he didn't quite know what to make of Sam. He was bright, accomplished, but always moaning about his troubles. Jason hated a whiner and Sam was the most talented and vocal whiner he had ever met. What was really strange was Sam's success. He was a leader in the industry with a wonderful wife and two sons, one, a doctor in research and the other an attorney working as a Supreme Court clerk. Yet, Sam moped around, bemoaning his fate in the world. It didn't make sense, and there was also the way he dressed; suit, tie, not what you'd expect in a high tech company where the geniuses dressed like homeless people. When he talked to Sam, it was always at a technical level that was stimulating. One point in favor of Sam's group was that Jason's best friend, a self-educated computer scientist, worked in the group and encouraged him to join. A chance to work alongside his friend was very tempting.

He took his exit and drove down several deserted side streets toward his one bedroom home. Each streetlight lit up his dashboard before dropping him into another uncomfortable darkness.

He had lived alone since his divorce and his dedication to his projects didn't really allow any room for a relationship. He had dated off and on, but he was preoccupied with work and couldn't seem to connect with anyone, at least, not yet.

Moira led the other group at Aquatech and she had also approached him during the last year about transferring to her group. She was a dynamo of energy, and her team was busy developing cloud computing applications that had the promise of revolutionizing the commercial world. But Moira was the most aggressive female he had ever encountered. Nothing stood in her way when she tackled an issue and there were several dead bodies, usually ex managers, in her wake. However, she had hired Charles onto her team, the software guru who had developed the Word and Excel applications for Microsoft. He was a multi-millionaire as well as a brilliant developer. Working in her group would mean the opportunity to work alongside Charles. It was also a very tempting offer.

As he unlocked his front door and stepped inside, he realized how hungry he was. A quick lunch and no dinner had left his internal engine running on empty. He woofed down a hamburger before sitting down to watch twenty minutes of brainless TV with a bottle of Heineken to help him wind down. He would think about his decision in the morning. When he couldn't keep his eyes open any longer, he went to bed. Seconds after his head hit the pillow, he was asleep.

He entered his second story flat. It was a row house, laid out just like his childhood home. On some semi-conscious level, he knew this was an eerie dream. He stopped inside in a hallway with unremarkable wallpaper. He moved down the hallway, cautiously. The flat was strange and hollow, no furniture and no sign of life. He went into a room with the same unremarkable wallpaper and hardwood floors. It felt desolate, the emptiness oppressive. He had a bad feeling about this place, but continued down the hall to the next room. It was also empty. The bad feeling surrounded him and weighed him down like quicksand. Something was missing. He looked around. Windows, the rooms had no windows.

At the doorway to the last room, he stopped. A large crate rested on the floor at the right side of this room. There was nothing else in the room, just the crate. He stepped closer. It wasn't a crate. It was a coffin, a wooden coffin. Curious and terrified at the same time, he felt compelled to see what was in the coffin, but at the same time, he feared what he might see. He moved and the floor creaked. Or was it the coffin that creaked? He stood over the coffin. Why was it here? Why was he here? What was it all about?

He knew he was supposed to look into the coffin, like there was a prime directive that he had to follow, but he didn't want to, he really, really didn't want to. He shook his head and started to back away, but as he did the lid of the coffin began to open, slowly. Transfixed, he froze. The shape inside was dressed in a white gown, a woman, her face cadaverous, horrible, grinning, two oversized bloody incisors exposed.

He took another step back, still shaking his head, this couldn't be happening. He looked down at her skeletal hands, clasped together at her waist, holding a dagger, the kind he had seen in Egyptian museums made with wavy metal, both sharp edges undulating in a snake-like pattern. The blade was covered with blood. He tried to breathe, but gagged, turned, ran out the door, then stopped and looked back. She was sitting up, rising out of the coffin. She was going to come after him. Before he could move, she was standing, moving toward him, fast, too fast.

Suddenly, wrapped in panic, he turned and ran down the hall, toward the back of the house, toward a door at the end of the hall. He grabbed the doorknob and glanced back. She was in the hallway, dagger raised, coming for him. He pulled the door open, took a step, but there was no floor, no step. He fell. Falling, he was falling, he screamed . . .

Jason sat up in bed and flicked the light on, still shaking. "No! No! No!" he said, aloud. Drenched in sweat, he wiped his face with the bed sheet. There was no question in his mind now. The decision was made. He would not go to work for Moira, for the vampire woman.

Toys

Jimmy's face flushed; his expression squeezed, voice raised, "You cheated!"

"Did not! You left your hover-tank in the open and my anti-grav-copter got him."

"You can't use kill-gas, Raymond. It's in the rules."

"My ion rocket torpedo did not have kill-gas."

"But it had a kill-gas symbol on the torpedo. I saw it."

"That was a flash-gas symbol. You know. It's like that old-fashioned napalm they used to use, except this vaporizes everything. Check it yourself. Just reverse the game back some screen scenes. You'll see."

Jimmy was sitting on his bed with sense-gauntlets on both hands and his virtual-reality goggles on. His best friend, Raymond, was not visible, but he knew he was there, hiding in a virtual command center. Jimmy left the three-dimensional war-game world and addressed the computer directly over his link, "Computer - game number 2-7-3-0-1. Slow, step, reverse." Then he watched as their war scenes stepped backwards. He saw the torpedo leaving Raymond's copter. He commanded, "Freeze." Raymond was right; it was the flash-gas symbol. He canceled out.

"Okay, Raymond. You're right. It was flash-gas." He paused, "Raymond."

"Yes."

"I don't want to play anymore."

"Shall we save the game?"

"No. Kill it. We'll start over next time."

"Okay. But keep your audio-video link live."

"Sure." Jimmy had played badly and he knew it. Sometimes he knew before they played that he would lose and it bothered him, like something was holding on to him, making him suffer through being a loser. He hated that feeling.

"Jimmy."

"Yeah." He looked over at Raymond's full sized image on the wall screen. Raymond was in his bedroom too, sitting in an overstuffed reading chair in the corner, his gauntlets and VR goggles lying on the floor next to him. He was three years older than Jimmy, a little taller, more filled out, wave in his hair, a natural athlete in the making. Raymond was sixteen years from insemination. Back when people used birth dates, that would have made him fifteen.

In school, Raymond seemed to excel at everything while Jimmy had to struggle. With schooling managed and taught on-line by a central national computer program, education was standardized, testing was standardized and grading was standardized, so each boy knew his ranking.

Raymond's room was nicer than his, framed posters, a long wrap-around desk, a skylight and several windows. Like everyone else, they had rooms that were fully network compatible and environmentally controlled.

Raymond stared, "You look like you lost your last toy. What's the matter?"

"Nothin'. Look, it's time for my fitness condition-
ing. I have to go. The exercise room will alert mom if
I don't show up"

Raymond said, "I think I know."

"Know what?"

"I think I know what's bothering you."

Jimmy didn't say anything, so Raymond continued, "It's about your dad."

"What about him?"

"Every time something about gas comes up, you
get this way. It's because your dad died in one of the
big terrorist gas attacks back in 2003."

"So what! I wasn't even born yet."

"Yeah, but you get weird whenever there is a gas
attack in the game. You miss him, don't you."

Jimmy didn't answer. Raymond watched his
best friend sitting on the bed, reddish hair, freckles,
gangly build, clothes scattered on the floor—a picture
of disorganization and dejection. He had to think of a
way to help him, "Jimmy."

"What?"

"Let's do something really crazy."

"Like what?"

"We're best friends, right?"

"Sure."

"Best friends trust each other, right?"

"Yeah."

"Do you trust me?"

"Well … yes."

"Okay. You know the road that is in front of your
house?"

"I've seen it on Super-Mapquest."

"Well, it goes in front of my house too."

"No kidding?"

"Right. So go down to the exercise room, log in some false times, then walk out to the road, turn left and walk to meet me."

"Go outside!"

"Yes."

"No one goes outside, Raymond. Outside is where you die. That's why we have totally self-contained houses. I can't do that."

"Yes, you can, Jimmy. Listen, I found this paper book about the old times."

"You mean a book with paper pages? I've never even seen one."

"People went outside … all the time. Kids went outside and played with toys, real toys that were not in a computer."

"Wow! I don't believe it."

"It's true. And people saw each other … in person … and they touched."

"Touched? Did they die then?"

"No, Jimmy. They didn't die, and we won't either. So we can walk out on our road and we can shake hands … in person … touching. Will you do it?"

"I don't know."

"I'm going out now. I'll wait for you on the road."

Raymond disappeared and the screen saver displayed. Jimmy sat still. He didn't want to scare his mom, but he knew she would never let him outside. And he thought, sometimes you have to take a chance. The muscles in his face took on a set; he stood, walked to the exercise room, set it for one hour, then continued to the exit chamber and stepped in. When the automatic air wash cycle finished, he reached for the outside door latch, and stepped outside. He heard the door lock behind him.

Water Event

I arrived for my third counseling session with Debbie. She was in one of those older brown-shingled downtown Los Gatos professional office buildings. Her office was on the second floor, up two flights of stairs and down a dark hallway. The waiting room was miniscule with two uncomfortable chairs, a miniature magazine rack and a small stereo playing elevator music to mask conversations with her clientele.

She opened the door to let a serious young couple leave and beckon me in, "How are you Frank?"

"It isn't my best week." I heard the somber tone in my own voice and wondered if I had suppressed feelings of sadness.

"Sit down and tell me about it." Debbie could read my feelings before I did, the main reason I chose to work with her.

The room was homey with one table lamp, an overstuffed settee for two clients, a swivel chair in case there was a third party and Debbie's chair. She already knew most of the details of my divorce, my child support payments, and the visitation arrangement with my three children. She also knew about the boy friend who replaced me. "I tried to see the kids again and she had ten more excuses for putting me off."

"Your court appointed visitation lets you see the kids every other weekend. Is that a problem?"

"It shouldn't be, but it always seems to be. This time it was her boyfriend's family emergency. The last time it was a previously planned trip out of town. It always seems to be something and she presents these activities to me as though the kids want to do them and they don't really want to see me anyway."

"Do you believe that?"

"No, not really. Well … I hope not."

"You don't seem sure."

"I want to be sure, but I guess I'm really not sure."

"We've talked about this."

"Yes. I know. I really do know they love me. I certainly love them. I just get to feeling bad and I can't seem to get over it."

"Your children need you and they need to know you are there for them. It's not financial support that is at issue for them, it is emotional support from you."

"I know that intellectually, but I feel like I'm in a dark hole and it's not a place that will let me provide support to anyone else. I can't even take care of myself."

Debbie paused to look at the clock she keeps on a table next to her chair, "Let's talk about work for a minute." "It's okay. They know I'm bummed and they leave me alone."

"Then you could take a short break?"

Shocked, my head spun. "You mean a vacation?"

"I mean a renewal. You need to find yourself before you can handle your ex, support your kids and continue your life. Forty isn't old Frank. You're healthy and fit, you like the outdoors, you're slightly graying, a distinguished attractive man. Women refer to men like you as a hunk."

"A hunk?"

"Don't worry about it. You just need to get a life. Is there something you have wanted to do or some place that you have always wanted to visit?"

And that's how I ended up on a Taca airline direct flight to Belize. The Stewardess shook me awake, leaning close to me in a cloud of her lovely cologne. "The Captain has announced our landing."

We exchanged smiles. I had dreamt I was dancing on the beach with a beautiful woman, her long blonde hair flowed over her shoulders like waves breaking on soft sand.

I remembered seeing photos of SCUBA dives around its 200 little islands and caves, so an escape to sub-tropical Belize was the first thing I thought of in Debbie's office. The country was small, approximately 180 miles long and 70 miles wide, with a population of 200,000 and it was an independent British Protectorate, so the official language was English, which made traveling and negotiating easier for American tourists.

Luckily, it was March, which avoided the soaring temperatures that begin in April, the heavy rains in May, and the hurricanes in August. We landed at the Philip S. Goldson International Airport, 10 miles outside Belize City, where I rented a car. I started out on the road toward Pine Lodge, a place I had picked because it was only five miles from the Mountain Pine Ridge Forest Reserve in the Cayo District, an ideal location for my first hike to its waterfalls.

As I left the city and its civilization, the road wound through typical Central American jungle—deep green on both sides of the road, huge ferns and foliage growing right to the edge of the paved roadway. The outside temperature indicator on the dash began to drop as I neared the Reserve. I turned off the AC, opened my driver's side window and felt the warm air on my arm and face, and accepted the fertile smell of raw growing things.

The jungle morphed into a forest of tall thin pines, the unique pine forest I had read about that only existed in this area of Central America. I reached Pine Lodge in about three hours, parked, grabbed my single suitcase and walked to the registration desk in the lodge building.

The small dark man behind the desk looked up as I set my case down, "Good evening sir."

"Good evening. My name is Frank Carter. I have a single reservation for a cottage with a private bath."

"Yes, sir. No problem sir. You have paid in advance. I can show you on our facility map where your cottage is located."

He circled a small square on the map and handed it to me. I stuffed it in my shirt pocket, "Thanks, but I was hoping to get something to eat. I came right from the airport and I'm starved. The snack on the plane was terrible."

"Yes sir, but it is past the dinner time. We no longer have cooks here this late."

"Oh boy! Just my luck. Do you have anything, some fruit or bread?"

"I can get you a mango, a lime and some flatbread."

"That will have to do. As soon as you can, please! I'm really hungry."

"Yes sir."

The little guy scurried back into an area that looked like an outdoor café with tables and disappeared. I followed and sat down at one of the tables. I had read that there was a great deal of ethnic diversity among Belizeans that included African-European, Spanish-Indian, African-Indian, Mayan, Anglo-European, Middle Eastern and Asian. So I had no idea what ethnicity my small dark friend was, but it didn't really matter as long as he brought me some food.

"Here, sir."

He appeared like magic, without a sound, and somehow, without my seeing him coming. It was a little spooky, but he had a dish, covered with mango slices, a couple of limes and three pieces of some flat-bread that looked like an irregular tortilla, "Thanks."

"You are welcome, sir."

The scent from the mango was sweet and amazing. I squeezed the limes on the mango, picked up a piece with my fingers and put it in my mouth. The first taste sent a wave of pleasure that made my eyes water. I wolfed down what was left with the bread and the plate was empty, it seemed, in minutes.

I sat at my table after I finished the food, just looking around, experiencing the environment and letting down from the trip. Home and all of my problems seemed to exist in some bad dream. This different world in front of me and its engaging newness temporarily masked my past problems, so I just left them hidden in some deep mental recess.

It was dark now. If there were any people here, they were probably asleep. I could hear a breeze high up in the trees, but the temperature hadn't dropped yet. It was still just about 80 degrees, maybe a little less and the air was sticky. Now that I was here and had eaten, I let the exhaustion come. I decided to find my cottage before I fell asleep in my chair.

I pulled out the small map that the man at the reception counter had given me, picked up my suitcase and walked back to the front of the lodge and around toward the building circled on the map. My cottage was a separate hut with some kind of thatch roofing. Inside were a bed, a small wooden dresser, a chair and a rack for clothes. It also had a shower, a small sink and a flush toilet. I took off my clothes, threw them over the rack, and got into bed. The last thing I remember was the smell of straw as I pulled the sheet up over me.

I sat straight up in bed. I could hear voices; it was hot; it was light and I was hungry again. I grabbed the same clothes, dressed and hurried outside. I couldn't afford to miss another meal. I walked to the café area and immediately smelled coffee.

There were people now, several couples, a few singles and the language was not all English. I sat down, and just like last night, a person appeared next to me without my noticing how he got there.

"Breakfast sir? Do you want coffee or tea?"

"Yes breakfast, please, and coffee quickly!"

"Yes sir."

Breakfast over, I took a quick shower and dressed for a warm day; cargo shorts, a loose Hawaiian shirt, sandals. I stopped at the kitchen to pick up the bag lunch that was prepared for me, a sandwich, mango slices and a baggie of trail mix. They had some trail maps at the front desk, my next stop.

Unfolding the map on the registration desk, "Is this the road to the Hidden Valley waterfall?"

"Yes sir. It is about nine miles east from the Reserve main entrance." He pointed to a small building symbol on the map. "You have 4-wheel drive?"

"Do I need 4-wheel drive?"

"In the Reserve, yes sir. Even in the best times it can rain heavily and the road becomes all mud. Regular 2-wheel drive autos are not recommended. The park rangers will not let you in without a 4-wheel drive."

"Damn! I missed that little piece of information. Well, I came all this way to see that waterfall and I'm damn well going to see it. Nine miles is an easy day's hike and I'll take my bedroll, stay over and hike out tomorrow. It is safe to stay at the falls?"

"There are no carnivores and there is a picnic bench by the falls."

"Good."

"A word. Sir, the staff here call the eddy under the falls, the Devil's Cauldron."

"Ha. I don't believe in superstitions."

"You are prepared for rain, sir?"

"I'll take my chances. Can you get me an extra bag lunch?"

"Yes sir. Just stop by the kitchen. They can make it for you in just a few minutes."

"Thanks."

My Minolta and REI pack in the back of the car with insect repellant, two lunches, extra water and a light bedroll, I parked at the entrance to the Reserve, checked in with the rangers and started down the road. I was going to have to make good time to get to the waterfall in time for a swim. It was already 11 am local time. I should be able to make it by about 4 pm.

I locked a 300 mm telephoto lens on my camera body, loaded film and I was ready to go.

It was not long before the road in this strange mix of jungle and pine forest turned to muck and I realized why they insist on 4-wheel drive vehicles. I scanned the area on both sides of the road as I hiked hoping to catch sight of one of the animals unique to the area, which I had read included jaguarundi, kinkajou, paca, armadillo, and iguana. I even stopped at a few places, remaining immoble, thinking that standing quietly might allow me to spot an animal, but I didn't see anything. Bird calls followed me and announced my intrusion—maybe it was a warning system to their friends.

Two 4-wheel drive vehicles passed me on their way to the waterfall. Although called the Hidden Valley Falls, it is referred to locally as the 1,000-foot waterfall, a fact, which is interesting primarily because it is higher, a full 1,500 feet high.

I clicked off a couple of frames on a toucan and some more on a spider monkey, but I didn't see any cats. The more exotic animals were in the lower elevation tropical jungles, probably better for me to have a carefree overnight at the falls.

It got warmer as I dropped lower in elevation toward the Belize River and the bottom of the falls. About two o'clock I stopped to take my pack off and sit on a fallen tree trunk along the road where I pulled out my first lunch. I didn't realize how hungry I was until I unwrapped that chicken sandwich. The taste was different, tangier than the chicken breast at home. For just a moment, I worried whether it might be too old, going bad, but it looked good. The hell with it,

I thought, and wolfed it down. The mango slices were a wonderful dessert, a heavy sweet perfume as I opened the package, even better than the night before, the warmth of the day releasing the flavor.

It felt good to just sit on the log and watch the bugs I didn't recognize navigate the forest floor. I could see the flap of wings in the trees, but it was too dense to make out what type of bird it was. Now that I wasn't moving or making noise or breathing loudly, the forest was filled with sounds, not all birds, but not distinguishable to me.

How different this was from the forests at home, the hiking in the Sierras and even some of the hiking I had done in Hawaii wilderness areas on the north coast of Kauai. I remembered the warm beaches, the hot trails and the tepid water along the shores. Inadvertently my eyes drooped; I jerked myself upright. Jesus, I thought, I'm falling asleep sitting here on this log. The time zone change, the travel, the strange bed and today charging out on this hike—my body was giving me a weariness message; time to move on, Frank. And now I was talking to myself.

I forced myself up, swung my pack on and adjusted the straps. It was already three o'clock. I had burned a whole hour in aimless reverie sitting on that log.

After another hour of hiking mostly down, I spotted a strange shape growing in the crotch of a nearby tree. I unclipped my camera from its case and pushed through the brush toward it. It was a bromeliad. I had read they were here in jungle areas, but I didn't expect to see one on this road. I clicked off two shots and started back down the road.

It was just plain hot now. I had drunk about a third of my water and my clothes were wet through with sweat. The road end and turnaround was just ahead and as I reached it, I could see two trailheads marked, one to the bottom of the falls. Both SUVs that had driven in had already left and passed me on their way out. The parking area was empty. It was about 5:30 pm and all I could think about was immersing myself in a cool pool. I began to realize how exhausted I really was and I berated myself for not just taking a day off to adjust to the time, the altitude and the heat. But I had been planning this two-week vacation for months and I couldn't wait to get here and I wanted to do it all while I was here. So I was doing it, tired or not.

Forty-five minutes later I got to Hidden Valley Falls and stood in awe, looking up to the top of the falls in waning daylight, where water shot out off the cliff edge and dropped 1,500 feet to the pool formed in the igneous rock formation where I was standing. Behind me was a flat spot next to the forest with a single picnic table. A small backpacking tent was off to the side. Someone was here, but not in the tent.

The rock pool was a jagged circle, several feet high with an outlet eroded at the downstream side. The water had pounded away at the rock for millions of years and chiseled out a deep pool. The sound was constant, not the roar of a wide waterfall, but the thinner, high pitched steady splash of a hundred water faucets. I dropped my pack, pulled off my clothes and climbed down to the edge of the pool. I felt the coolness of the water on my feet and my body anticipated the caress and rejuvenation of total immersion.

I leaned forward and sagged into the pool, engaging the water along the length of my body like the launching of some great ship. Under the surface the stirring and spinning water touched me and petted me like a hundred mermaids with feather hands. I surfaced, breathed and sank into the water again, breast stroking toward the falling water, imagining myself cleansed by tumbler action like a limp sweat suit in a washing machine. I let the circular motion take control, feeling the power of the current. Then, when I tried to swim out, I realized I was in trouble ......

∼

I was in trouble, trapped in an eddy, arms felt leaden, water pounding down, rocks wet, slippery and I couldn't get out; no idea how long I had been in the water. I took a breath, went down, and tried to rest my arms; hoping to break the fatigue; it didn't work. I just kept getting tired. It was quiet under the water—safe—restful—I could just stay here—all my problems resolved. I wondered if this was how drowning felt. Dream images formed; looking down into the pool, I watched my flaccid, dead body spinning in the eddy, face down, dark brown hair swirling; then dragged onto the rocky beach by two men, face a ghoulish white; then in a coffin, candle lit, my muscled tan arms folded over my stomach; no! no! no!

I came up for air again and saw a woman wearing a cowboy hat and holding a leather strap tied to a horse, standing on the rocks above me. All I could get out was, "Rope!" before I slipped under. I made another conscious effort to get my head above water. It seemed like an immense effort. I broke the surface.

She cupped her hands over her mouth and yelled over the splashing waterfall, "Are you in trouble?"

"Yes! Rope! My pack! Help!" and I slipped under again. I could see the surge of bubbles churning under the waterfall as the force of the eddy whipped me down and I forced myself to struggle up again, just one more time I thought, just one more time. I got my right hand out of the water, then my mouth and nose; I sucked in air. I saw her spinning the rope over her head like a lasso.

"Grab it!" She yelled and the rope hit my right hand. I grabbed the rope, first with my right, and then immediately also with my left, savoring the help, breathing, not sinking down again.

She said, "Easy does it. Not so fast. I'll guide you to the edge. "Okay. Thanks."

"Save your breath. I'm pulling you toward the lowest edge of rock. It will be easiest to get out there."

"Easy now, Molly." She patted the horse's neck.

I suddenly realized she was talking to a horse. She wrapped her end of the rope three times around the saddlehorn and backed the horse, pulling the rope taught. She patted the horse again. "Good girl. Stay there, Molly."

I gripped the rope like the lifeline it was. Near the lowest edge, I place one hand on the rock ledge, "I think I need help."

She leaned over me; hands under both arms and helped me straight up. I clambered over her and collapsed on the rock ledge next to her. Neither of us moved, but I was surprised by her strength. She read my thoughts and said, "Fitness is a benefit of working a ranch."

I realized I was sitting there nude, and tried to cover myself.

She laughed. "I've got two brothers and we're a working ranch, so don't worry, I've seen it all. You're shaking; maybe a little shocky. I'm going to get a blanket."

"I'll get dressed. That way we can share the blanket."

I watched her walk to the tent and come back with a blanket, "Thanks. Boy, am I glad you were here."

"No problem. How do you feel?"

"Like I wish I were home in bed and could sleep forever."

She laughed, a nice sound, "What are you doing out here?"

"It's my renewal and I was going for broke."

"You almost did, break that is. You've stopped shaking. Maybe a little food or something to drink would help."

"I've got water and another sandwich in my pack."

"Just sit there for a minute. I'll get it."

She brought them both, but when I looked at the water, I said, "I've had enough water for a while." It was my last sandwich but this was not a time for restraint, so I unwrapped it and took a big bite.

She looked at the sandwich, "Looks good. What is it?"

"It's chicken."

"Chicken?"

"Yeah. The kitchen people at the lodge called it bamboo chicken."

This brought on a big burst of laughing, during which she almost couldn't even say, "Oh, they did."

"What's so funny?"
"You. You don't know what bamboo chicken is."
"It's not chicken?"
"No. It's iguana lizard meat."
We both laughed at that.

The 25-Cent Murder

Detective Joe Moore sat in a booth in the Jury Room, the local tavern and hangout for attorneys, cops and the press. A dark hideout, it sat directly across from the Hall of Justice in the old part of downtown.

An attractive waitress picked up Joe's empty and set his second Corona on the table. He tipped his head as a salute. "Thanks babe."

He sipped the Corona, then set the bottle down and watched her ass as she walked back to the bar. He wiped a finger through the condensation running down the side of the bottle. Friday nights were boring without a woman, he thought.

Sean's voice broke his focus. "Hi, Joe. Checking out the scenery?"

"Leave it alone, Sean. I thought you'd show up. Have a seat."

As Sean slid into the booth across from him, Joe observed his friend. Although in his mid-thirties, Sean looked like a college kid, tall, lean, and hyper, the opposite of his friend, Joe.

Joe was closing on 50 and it showed in his paunch and the sprinkle of steel gray in his hair. As a detective, he wanted to observe and not be observed, so he dressed for the job in dark slacks, standard white shirt, blue-gray tie, and the dark blue windbreaker that he wore everywhere. He looked like anybody, inconspicuous, but he collected facts like a vacuum cleaner, seeing more than anyone else through his thick glasses.

Sean waved at the waitress, then turned back toward Joe. "I was hoping you might have something for me. I need a story for our Sunday series on cold cases." The waitress stopped at their booth. Without looking up, Sean said, "Guinness in a can, and bring a frosted glass."

Joe handed her his empty. She smiled at him. "Another?"

He smiled back. "Yeah." He leaned over to watch her walk away.

Sean's eyebrows rose. "A favorite of yours?"

Joe answered deadpan, "Maybe." His voice trailed off.

Sean caught his eye. "What's going down at the precinct? Anything juicy?"

Joe leaned against the back of the booth and curled his upper lip. "Same ole stuff. If they're stupid, they're in jail. If they're smart, they're still outside."

"No big cases?"

"Nope. Boring. Just the way I like it."

Joe was cantankerous; a real pain, but Sean liked his honesty and his encyclopedic memory. With Joe, there was never any bull. Truth was his personal penchant, his foil against evil.

The waitress returned, balancing a full tray while she transferred Joe's Corona and the can of Guinness with a glass to their table. The place was filling up with the after-work crowd from the Hall.

"What about past crimes, Joe. Any real interesting cold cases?"

"You've been around. You know what's gone down here."

Sean popped the top, tipped the glass and poured his Guinness, while watching the chocolate-colored currents swirl in the glass. "Only for the last five or six years. How about before then? What was your first tough case? You made detective fifteen years ago. That's a lot of water under one bridge."

Joe sipped his Corona, set it down in a different place and moved the little napkin over on the ring it left. "Well, there was one interesting case." He fingered the label on the Corona and started to peel it off slowly, engrossed in the process.

"Okay, Joe. I'm gettin' old waiting. Give."

"Gimme a break," Joe snapped. "It was a long time ago. Anyway, I tagged this case as the twenty-five-cent murder."

"Great headline! What did twenty-five cents have to do with it?"

"Hang on. You'll find out. The victim's name was Charles Bingham."

"I know that name. He was the town poet laureate back in the early 80's."

"Yeah, the same, and an English professor. He was rolling in inherited money, and he was a total ass to boot."

"Sounds like a charmer."

Joe's face tightened and flushed red. "Are you gonna keep interrupting me?"

"Touchy. You need another beer?"

"Don't piss me off, Sean."

"Okay, Okay. Go on with the story."

Joe paused, his eyes narrowed, but he continued,

"Bingham's housekeeper reported the death after she discovered him lying on the kitchen floor. He was fine two days earlier when he told her about the extra cleaning he wanted done. According to the coroner the cause of death was an exotic poison that was odorless and tasteless with a name I don't remember. But here's where the case got interesting. Forensics placed the death on Saturday night between 8 pm and midnight. A grease spot on his pants was identified as animal fat, specifically butter and even more specifically it was unsalted butter. Then the autopsy report came in listing the contents of his stomach. They estimated he had a large dinner, probably around six or seven o'clock. It looked like food residue from a normal dinner except for one thing, pomegranate seeds."

"Pomegranate seeds?"

"Weird, huh. I didn't think anyone ate those things. We used to give them to the pigs. But they were in this guy's stomach."

Sean shrugged. "Some people eat the whole pomegranate. It's not that rare."

Joe glared at him. "You wanna tell this story?"

Sean shook his head. "No." Joe picked up his Corona. Sean watched him over the rim of his glass. Finally, he said, "Okay, I give up. Why did you call this the twenty-five-cent murder?"

Joe finished his beer and sat back with a smirk on his lips. "When the coroner examined the body, he found a twenty-five-cent piece still clenched in Bingham's hand. He included it in his report but didn't think anything of it."

"What did you make of it?

"Nothing right away. The coin was just a standard 1995-quarter. Then we decided that he might have been trying to give us a clue and since the quarter was money, we did the usual thing, that is . . . we followed the money. And sure enough, he had three heirs. The money was to be divided evenly so they all became suspects."

Sean sipped his Guinness. "Who needed the money the most?"

"That wasn't clear in the beginning. All the heirs were children of Bingham's sister. She and her husband had both died in a small plane crash and they left a pretty hefty insurance payoff to Bingham, which, according to his current will, would pass through to the three heirs upon Bingham's death. But none of the three obviously needed the money. They were all single career people, a vice president in a mercantile company, a professor of philosophy and a real estate attorney, the only woman."

It was almost 5 pm; hot hors d'oeuvres were set out on the bar and the Jury Room was wall-to-wall noise, a cacophony of too many voices, fueled by too many drinks. The waitress stopped by, picked up their empties and waited, tapping her foot.

Sean, leaning forward, arms on the table, didn't notice her. "I'll bet on the professor. Graduates with a degree in philosophy supply the staffing for fast food restaurants. Even if he teaches, he makes a pittance compared to a VP and a lawyer."

Still standing there, the waitress put one hand on her hip. "Gentlemen? Do you need anything?"

Against the riot of background noise, Joe didn't hear her. "Not true for this duck. The professor published a ton of books, did lecture tours and invested his money well. He was definitely not suffering."

The waitress shrugged, mumbled "jerks!" under her breath and left.

Joe straightened up. "Shit!"

Sean watched her thread through the crowd, then he turned back to Joe. "You really do like her."

"Leave it alone, Sean."

"She'll be back." Sean reached in his pocket. "I'm buying." He put a twenty-dollar bill on the table and continued, "Poison is a woman's weapon, so I'll change my bet to the lawyer."

"Come on! That stereotype went out with Agatha Christie."

"Well then who was it?"

"God damn it. Do you want to hear this story or not?"

"Sorry. Go on."

"We interrogated all three of them separately and they all clammed up. No one would say anything, and they all wanted to see their lawyers first. In the meantime, we learned from Bingham's housekeeper that he never ate at home and only ate at one restaurant, but he didn't eat there that night. She remembered that he had been invited to a dinner party. So we canvassed all the catering or serving companies in the area searching for one that served a dish with pomegranates. We found a company that had served a private dinner at the VP's house on the Saturday night in question. The two people who worked the job gave us a description of the four people who were there, the three heirs and Bingham. Not only that, they gave us the menu for the dinner and guess what was served?"

"Sweet butter."

"Yes, but even more telling was another item, persimmon flan."

"It sounds like a dessert."

"Yeah. Guess what it's made with."

Sean tapped his fingers on the table. "I'm waiting patiently."

"You're such a wise ass, Sean! Anyway persimmon flan is made with sugar, water, persimmons, flour, cream cheese, eggs, milk and ... are you paying attention? "

"Yes?"

"Pomegranate seeds."

"Wow!"

"Yes. That placed all three of them purportedly at the scene of the crime, with the victim, hours before his death, and potentially able to slip him the poison. However, none of them had a unique motive, other than that they all hated him. When we confronted them with the dinner scene, they admitted to arranging the dinner so they could talk to old Bingham and stop him from changing his will to give everything to charity. But when it came to who gave him the poison, all three just shook their heads."

"Could all three have done it?"

"*Murder on the Orient Express*? There you go with another Agatha Christie reference. Maybe it was a conspiracy, but I don't think so. I'm sure that one of them did it, but all three gained by his death, so nobody was talking."

"An unsolved case."

"That's right, almost."

"What do you mean, almost?"

"I know who did it, but I can't prove it."

"What makes you think you know?"

"The clue Bingham left us."

"The quarter?"

"That's right. Remember Bingham was smart, and he was dying and he probably only had a few minutes during which he recognized that he had been poisoned and he was a goner. Remember also that Bingham was a poet, a good old-fashioned poet who liked rhyming poems."

"I still don't get it."

"What's on a quarter, a 1995 quarter?"

"Ben Franklin."

"The other side."

"An eagle."

"What rhymes with eagle?"

The waitress stopped back by their booth and answered, "Legal," as she scooped up both empties.

Both men looked up, mouths agape.

One hand on her hip, she looked Joe in the eye. "Well, it *does*."

Acknowledgements

Thanks to my daughter Siobhan Markee, who edited this book and made this publication possible, to my wife who has cheered me on through the tough times and the hard work it takes to publish a book, and to all the writers who encouraged me to keep writing.

About the Author

B orn and raised in San Francisco, Charles spent his boyhood summers wandering the hills, creeks and forests of northern California. After graduating from the University of California in Berkeley, he joined the Bay Area technology explosion, a choice that helped him support and raise a family of six boys and three girls. With his family grown, he left Silicon Valley in 2001 to forge a career in creative writing, publishing five books:

Other World Tales 1: Irish the Demon Slayer
Other World Tales 2: Demon Invasion
Other World Tales 3: The Ultimate Battle
Maria's Beads
A Conflicted Heart and Other Stories

www.ingramcontent.com/pod-product-compliance
Lightning Source LLC
Chambersburg PA
CBHW072001170626
46813CB00005B/1961